The Magnificent Challenge

Also by Dorothy Brenner Francis
in Large Print:

Keys to Love
A Blue Ribbon for Marni
The Legacy of Merton Manor
Murder in Hawaii
Nurse Under Fire

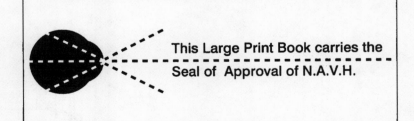

This Large Print Book carries the
Seal of Approval of N.A.V.H.

The Magnificent Challenge

Dorothy Brenner Francis

Thorndike Press • Waterville, Maine

Published in 2004 by arrangement with
Maureen Moran Agency.

Thorndike Press® Large Print Candlelight.

The text of this Large Print edition is unabridged.
Other aspects of the book may vary from the original edition.

Set in 16 pt. Plantin by Al Chase.

Printed in the United States on permanent paper.

Library of Congress Control Number: 2004041207
ISBN 0-7862-6389-X (lg. print : hc : alk. paper)

The
Magnificent
Challenge

As the Founder/CEO of NAVH, the only national health agency solely devoted to those who, although not totally blind, have an eye disease which could lead to serious visual impairment, I am pleased to recognize Thorndike Press⋆ as one of the leading publishers in the large print field.

Founded in 1954 in San Francisco to prepare large print textbooks for partially seeing children, NAVH became the pioneer and standard setting agency in the preparation of large type.

Today, those publishers who meet our standards carry the prestigious "Seal of Approval" indicating high quality large print. We are delighted that Thorndike Press is one of the publishers whose titles meet these standards. We are also pleased to recognize the significant contribution Thorndike Press is making in this important and growing field.

Lorraine H. Marchi, L.H.D.
Founder/CEO
NAVH

⋆ Thorndike Press encompasses the following imprints: Thorndike, Wheeler, Walker and Large Pr int Press.

Chapter One

Jess Wong fastened her seat belt as the jet roared toward the Honolulu airport. Peering through the plane window she saw only sun-washed sky and bottle-green sea, but the stewardess had said they would be landing soon. Oahu lay somewhere in the choppy waters below.

What would her father be like? Jess tried to imagine this parent whom she had never seen. The divorce had taken place when she was just a baby, and her mother had raised her in New York City. But her father had written to her through the years. He had sent pictures of himself and of the islands. He had sent her pearly shell necklaces and pikake perfume, and in Jess's mind he was a combination of Santa Claus, Marco Polo, and Confucius.

Her father had financed her college education, and now for the first time he had invited her to visit him. Jess pulled his latest letter from her purse and studied it as if it might contain some revealing secret that she had missed on other readings.

Dear Jess,

I hope you will accept this invitation to visit Malia and me. I may as well be honest with you. I want you to come live here in the islands at least for a while. Malia has always wanted to meet her sister, and needless to say I've often yearned to know my eldest daughter.

A person who has earned a teaching certificate has no business wasting her time working as a waitress. I know from your letters that your big desire is to be self-supporting and independent. I'm sorry that no teaching positions are available to you at this moment. But that's why I'm writing.

I can offer you a job here at Pine Pack. A pineapple cannery may be far removed from the classroom, but the job I have in mind involves creative work in public relations. It will be a good background for anything you may choose to do later. Of course, if a teaching job should open up, I would want you to take it if you so desired.

Please accept the enclosed check to cover your transportation costs, and please let me know when you'll arrive. Malia and I will meet you at the airport.

Love,
Dad

Jess refolded the letter and slipped it back into her purse. She wondered about both her father and her half-sister. Would they like her? Would she like them? But now there was no more time to worry about the wisdom of her decision to come to the islands. The plane touched down, bounced once, then touched down again and rolled to an easy stop on the concrete runway. A vast ocean lay like a barrier between her and her past life.

Deplaning took but a few minutes. Jess was the next to last person to pass through the exit, and she stood on the elevated ramp for a moment, drinking in the tropical scene. She inhaled the fresh scent of the sea breeze as she felt the mid-afternoon sun warm her head and shoulders. Hawaii! Descending the metal steps, she hurried to board a green and white wiki-wiki bus, which whisked her and other passengers to the baggage-claim area.

"Jess!" her father called to her, his voice resonate as a bass viol. "I would have known you anywhere."

"H-hello, Dad." Jess recognized her father from the pictures he had sent, but shyness overcame her and she could hardly speak. Should she shake hands with her father, or should she give him a hug? Before she could make up her mind, he slipped a white carnation lei over her head and planted a welcoming kiss on her cheek.

"How lovely!" Jess smiled into the dark eyes that were on a level with her own as she inhaled the spicy scent of the lei. She had thought her father would be tall, but he was of medium height. He was muscular and casually elegant in silk slacks and sport shirt. Although he had a playful glint in his eye that no camera had caught, there was a restlessness about him, an urgency that made itself felt.

"Jess, I want you to meet your sister, Malia." Her father stepped aside and nodded toward a pretty girl dressed in an ankle-length muumuu, who had kept in the background.

Jess smiled as Malia slipped a jade vine lei over her head and arranged it to fit inside the carnation lei already in place.

"Aloha, Jess. Welcome to the islands."

"Malia!" Jess stood back and gazed down at this girl with the silvery voice who was her half-sister, and suddenly she realized that they looked quite a bit alike. They both had inherited their father's dark skin and eyes and ebony-colored hair, and they both had his oval-shaped face. But there the resemblance ceased. Malia was short and rather thin, and her straight black hair hung almost to her waist. She looked like one of the beautiful girls on the Come To Hawaii posters. Almost as if by reflex, Jess touched her own short shag cut and straightened to her full five feet nine inches. Then Jess realized that she was staring at Malia. She smiled. "We have a lot of getting acquainted to do, haven't we?"

"Yes," Malia said. "And I'm looking forward to it. Dad's told me so much about you, and sometimes he shared your letters with me. I hope you'll like the islands."

"I already love them."

"We'd better pick up your bags and get on back to the house," Mr. Wong said. "Ora, our housekeeper, is dying to meet you."

Jess hurried to the revolving baggage platform and pointed out her suitcases. They each picked up one, then Jess and Malia fol-

11

lowed their father to a sleek black car in the visitors' parking area. They all sat in the front seat, and Jess gazed about in delight as her father eased the car into the traffic.

"There's so much to see that I know I'll miss something," she said.

"I'll play tour guide." Malia grinned up at her. "We're headed toward Waikiki Beach. You can see Diamond Head rising toward the sky."

"I've seen lots of pictures of it," Jess said. "Were there ever diamonds up there?"

"Long ago British sailors found sparkling stones in the hills, but they turned out to be calcite crystals. Yet the name 'diamond' stuck. Here's the Aloha Tower. It overlooks Honolulu harbor. You'll see lots of big ships anchor here. The *Canberra* is due soon. It's one of the largest luxury liners that stop regularly."

Jess looked at the harbor, then she gazed inland. "Can you tell me about the trees we're passing? I recognize the palms and banana trees, but what are some of the others?"

"The ones that look as if they have pineapples hanging from the branches are called pandanus trees. Ahead and to our left are some papaya trees." Malia inhaled deeply. "Do you smell the cannery?"

Jess sniffed. "Fresh pineapple. It smells wonderful. Is it like this all the time?"

"A lot of the time," Malia replied. "Are you going to drive by the plant, Dad?"

"Not now," Mr. Wong replied. "By the time we get home and Jess unpacks, it'll be the dinner hour. I know Ora's prepared a feast."

As they drove across the city Malia pointed out hibiscus, orchids, plumeria, until at last they turned onto a quiet road where the houses sat far apart in huge expanses of green lawn.

"Here we are." Mr. Wong turned into a circular driveway, braked the car to a stop in front of a redwood ranch-style home, and stepped onto the concrete. As if on signal, the front door of the house flew open and a tiny butterfly of a woman, dressed in an apricot-colored uniform and wearing golden hoop earrings and charm bracelets on both arms, stood gazing at them.

As they approached her, Mr. Wong said, "Jess, I want you to meet Ora Thane. She's been with the family for fifteen years, and we couldn't do without her."

"Hello, Ora," Jess said. "I'm glad to know you."

"That you have come, it is good." Ora smiled. Her high, whispery voice reminded

13

Jess of tinkling wind chimes and she waited to hear more, but Ora stood aside to let them enter the house.

Jess thought that she had never seen such a lovely home. Bare floors waxed to a gloss finish glowed in the hallway and the living room, and bamboo furniture with bright-colored cushions gave a cool, airy touch to the room. But Ora allowed them no time to linger.

"Follow me," she ordered. "Your room, she is waiting. Hope you will like."

Jess's father and sister carried her luggage to her room, then they excused themselves.

"I'll see you at dinner," her father said, restlessly slapping the fist of his right hand into the palm of his left hand.

"And I'll be right across the hall in case you need anything," Malia smiled. "Take your time unpacking. Dinner's not until six."

Jess felt all but overwhelmed as her new-found family left her alone. She had guessed that her father was wealthy, but she had not expected a mansion like this. And it was a mansion; yet it was different from any house she had ever seen. No heavy carpeting, no bulky furniture absorbed the heat. All the furnishings were as light and airy as the tradewinds that cooled the house.

For a moment Jess stood admiring the

simplicity of her room and relaxing in the cool blue-greens of the decorator's scheme. Then she circled the room, touching the single bed, the desk, the rattan chairs, and the combination bureau and vanity table that comprised the room's furnishings. She ran her fingers over them all as if they might disappear as a dream would. But this was no dream. Louvered doors hid an ample closet along one wall, and on the other side of the room sliding glass partitions opened onto an outdoor patio.

Pulling the green draperies aside and opening the sliding doors, Jess felt that she was living in an outdoor room. A plumeria tree dropped pink blossoms on the lava rock patio, and she inhaled their sweet fragrance. She hated to go back inside, to get to the business of unpacking, but she forced herself to do it. Once her clothes hung in the closet this paradise would seem more like home. And she intended to make it her home, for the time being at least.

As she arranged her things carefully in drawers and on shelves, Jess tried to squelch the memory of the sadness in her mother's voice when she had announced her plans to visit her father. Yet her mother had been fair. There had been no bitter words. Her mother had wished her well.

Through the years Jess's mother had expressed her disapproval of her ex-husband in subtle ways. She had dropped casual but caustic comments about his big-business ventures, his country-club life-style, and his restlessness. Jess now wondered how much had been truth and how much imagination.

"All unpacked?" Malia poked her head through the doorway, breaking into Jess's thoughts.

"Unpacked enough for the time being. I'll leave the details until tomorrow." Jess glanced at Malia's bright-hued caftan and the golden slippers that peeked from beneath it. She suddenly felt out of place in her simple tailored sheath. "Do you dress for dinner? I'm afraid I've brought nothing. . . ."

"You look fine," Malia said. "This is just the casual costume of the islands. I love long dresses, so I wear them most of the time. If you'd like one, we'll go on a shopping spree soon. But right now I'll give you a tour of the house before Ora serves dinner."

Jess followed Malia down the hallway. Her sister walked slowly and gracefully, like a dancer moving across a stage.

"The house is U-shaped," Malia explained. "On this wing are three bedrooms, yours, mine, and Ora's. Then on the bottom

16

of the U we have the living room, dining room, and a family room, which you caught a glimpse of when you arrived."

Jess peeked at those three rooms again as they passed through the hallway. Everything was elegantly casual, light, and airy.

"The other side of the U houses Dad's office and bedroom and my studio," Malia explained.

"What sort of a studio do you have?" Jess asked.

"I'll show it to you." Malia quickened her pace, and her caftan made soft, swishing sounds. "I'm a violinist and I have a teaching studio here at the house. But you needn't worry. It's soundproof. My students will come and go and you will never hear them."

"Oh, but I'd love to hear them," Jess said.

"Of course, you may listen if you wish." Malia's laugh floated like a flute scale, and she shrugged as she opened the door to a small studio. "The acoustical tiles absorb most of the sound. What they miss, the velvet draperies catch."

Jess blinked. The room was tastefully done, yet the shocking pink of the velvet draperies leaped at her. Music was scattered here and there on chairs and floor, and an electric metronome ticked an allegro beat until Malia reached to turn it off. Jess crossed the purple carpet and touched the ebony grand piano that stood in one corner of the room. The only other furnishings were music cabinets, music racks, and a huge desk and chair. A few framed certificates hung on the wall near Jess, awards for musical performances and even a certificate stating that Malia had completed a Red Cross first-aid class.

"Do you have many pupils?" Jess asked.

"Only thirty. You see, I'm still in college. I only teach part time. Then I also play in the Honolulu symphony orchestra."

Jess looked at her sister with new respect. Somehow she had imagined that Malia worked for their father at the cannery. Malia seemed untroubled over the untidy state of her studio. She closed the door on it and led the way on down the hall.

"I guess I want to have life two ways, Jess." Malia looked up at Jess. "I want marriage and a career. I think music and private teaching will combine nicely with family life."

"I suppose you're right," Jess said.

"Have you ever thought of getting married?" Malia asked.

"Not seriously." Jess hoped her abruptness would close that subject. She didn't want to share her views of marriage and of broken homes with this girl she hardly knew.

Pausing at the doorway to Mr. Wong's office, the girls looked inside.

"What a beautiful desk!" Jess said.

"It's made of monkeypod wood," Malia replied. "It's quite special. Dad's bedroom joins his office on the right. He works here at home when things get too hectic at the cannery. It gives him a change of scene, and it gives his co-workers a rest."

"You make him sound like a slave driver." Jess laughed.

"Oh, no," Malia said. "Dad's just a soaring spirit whom fortune accidentally dropped into an office. He loves Pine Pack, and for the most part he's a conservative businessman, but his mind takes flight sometimes. I'm sure he drives his secretary crazy — always coming up with a new idea for a fantastic filing system or a different use for carbon paper."

Jess was about to ask more about her father, but Ora darted down the hallway toward them.

"Dinner is served, Miss Malia, Miss Jess. Do come promptly. Your father is already in the dining room pacing a ring around the table."

In her apricot-colored uniform Ora again reminded Jess of an exotic butterfly, flitting from here to there. Willingly she followed her. She hadn't realized how hungry she was until Ora mentioned food.

"We'll eat on the dining lanai," Malia said, leading the way on through the dining room to the outdoor terrace. "We always eat out here unless it's raining. Too bad it's too soon to light the torches. But dinner's early tonight. I have to perform in the concert later in the evening. Perhaps you'd like to come listen."

Jess nodded as they stepped onto a lanai surrounded by palms and plumeria trees. Her father greeted them, then held their chairs for them as they seated themselves at the table. Four places were laid around a centerpiece of yellow hibiscus blossoms backed by a fan of green leaves. As soon as Ora brought the food to the table, she joined them and served the dinner family style. Jess tasted her iced tea which was spiked with a pineapple spear and found it delicious.

"Mahimahi is the fish you are eating," Ora said. "Is a specialty of the islands. The fruit salad has guava, papaya, and banana. Add lemon juice if you like."

"It's wonderful, Ora," Jess said.

"Ora's a great cook," Mr. Wong said. "Her real speciality is supreme baked chicken. My favorite."

"Is on menu for tomorrow, sir," Ora replied.

As soon as they finished eating their main course, Ora served macadamia nut ice cream and coconut cookies for dessert, then she excused herself. Once she was gone, Mr. Wong began to talk business.

"Jess, what do you know about public relations?"

"Not much, I'm afraid, Dad. But I did read some books on the subject after I received your invitation."

"It's a concept too big to be captured in a book," her father said.

"Dad," Malia interrupted. "If you two will excuse me, I'll go dress for the concert. Jess, I'll stop back for you in a half-hour. Okay? Of course if you don't want to go . . ."

"But I do want to go. That is if it's okay with everyone." She looked at her father, who nodded his approval.

Malia left the lanai, and Mr. Wong said, "You have a good education, Jess, but always remember that imagination is more important than knowledge. I'm seeking people who think differently for my public relations staff at Pine Pack."

Jess nodded. "What will my job be? Public relations sounds like a glamor field to me."

"PR people work for good will. They tell what's good about Pine Pack. I'm concerned with improving relationships between our cannery and the public on which it depends. You may call it a glamor business if you want to. In a way it is. Eventually you will work with the media, newspaper men and women, magazine editors and writers, radio and TV people. But at first you'll work with humdrum daily routine."

"It all sounds fascinating," Jess said. "But can you give me a hint as to what I'll actually be doing? Frankly I'm scared to bits. What if I can't handle the job?"

"At first you'll be the odd-job girl. I think I'll have you start rewriting a brochure about Pine Pack that will be given to all employees. It will outline the various jobs in the cannery, and it will give a brief history of the company."

"Sounds like a great way for me to learn the business from the inside out," Jess said.

"Right." Her father nodded, then his face clouded and he squirmed in his chair. "There're two things, two special things that I'm going to ask you to do. You may not like them. First I want you to change your name."

Jess stared at her father. What was this

man, this stranger, up to? "What sort of a change?"

"Just go by your first and middle names. Jess Merrill. I want no one to know that you're my daughter."

Jess scraped her chair back from the table and clenched her fists. "If you're ashamed of me, you shouldn't have asked me here. I'm not seeking charity. I had a job on the mainland, not a very good job, I'll admit. But I was independent. I don't need your wealth. You can't buy me."

"Hold on! Hold on!" Her father jumped up and began pacing. "I'm certainly not trying to buy you. I'm a wealthy man, true. But I've tried to use my wealth for the good of society — for the good of the islands. That has always been my dream. I want you to drop Wong from your last name for a very special reason."

Jess felt herself blushing and she regretted sounding off before she had all the facts.

"I'm sorry, Dad. I really am. But your invitation to come here to work came to me as a big surprise. I could hardly believe it was true, and I keep expecting a catch of some sort. I'll use my middle name if it will serve some good purpose."

"I need someone I can trust, Jess. It's true that I represent wealth and big business. My father studied war and politics so I could study mathematics and commerce. And as a result I've succeeded in business. But I've done it to glorify the islands and to make it possible for my daughters to be musicians and teachers."

"I don't understand." Jess wished that she knew her father better. "What can I do for you that any other employee couldn't do?"

"Public relations information from the Pine Pack office is leaking to our opponent, Commercial Can. My PR people come up with good ideas for promoting Pine Pack, but before our ideas get beyond the planning stage, Commercial Can is using them. This sort of thing has to stop, and I'm counting on you to help stop it. As a new employee you are apt to be approached concerning the information leaks. So far I've treated the leaks as coincidences. But I know better. In about three months I want to launch a special public relations campaign. I want you to help me find the guilty person, the person who is trying to undermine our company, before that time."

"That sounds like a big order," Jess said. "I don't know where I'd start. Whom do you suspect?"

"There are three employees in the public relations office. It has to be one of them.

Your job is to find out which one."

"Who are the three? I don't like the idea of spying on people. I don't know if I can handle such a job."

"Whether or not you believe you can do a thing, you are right." Her father paused to let his words sink in. Then he sat down once more. "If my guess is correct it won't take long to learn where the leak is. The three employees in the office are Johnny Kuhio, editor of the company newspaper; Reeta McQuigg, a general PR worker; and Alex Yanagisako, the head of the office."

"What sort of information has leaked out?" Jess asked.

Her father drummed on the table with his fingertips. "Well, there was the TV show we had planned to broadcast on the mainland, where most of our customers are. The show was one of a family comedy series, and the basic plot concerned a young wife who in the beginning months of her pregnancy craved pineapple in the middle of the night. Pine Pack's only screen credit was to be our trademark, the smiling pineapple emblem, which was to appear at the grocery counter where the husband purchased the pineapple."

"Sounds like a great idea," Jess said. "Sort of a soft-sell approach."

"Right!" Mr. Wong jumped to his feet again. "But before the show was produced a similar program appeared on another network. Only this time the credit went to Commercial Can. The leak must have come from my own office. Of course our program was canceled, and we were left back where we started — searching for the big new idea that would present Pine Pack in a favorable light."

"But what motive would your own public relations employees have for leaking ideas to the opponents?" Jess asked.

"I wish I knew." Her father paced and scowled. "I wish I knew. Johnny Kuhio is rather a beach bum type who openly resents big business. He could be the one. He runs with a bunch of longhaired surfers who've never earned a dime, yet they think they should have the right to run the world. When they earn the right, then I'll listen to them."

"Why did you hire him if that's his attitude?" Jess asked.

"More public relations." Her father laughed. "I like to cooperate with the university. Johnny's working on an advanced degree in journalism. In place of a thesis, he has elected to edit a company paper for one year with no salary. He works half-days —

mornings. The other half he's a beach boy for one of the big hotels."

"What about the other employees?" Jess asked. "Reeta McQuigg? Does she have a motive?"

"I wish I knew. Reeta comes from a society family — descendants of the first missionaries to land at Lahaina; and Alex Yanagisako is the son of one of the outstanding Japanese families on the islands. Either of these two might be selling our PR ideas to Commercial Can. There may be big money involved for all I know."

"Ready to go?" Malia stepped back into the room and peered at her watch.

"She's ready," their father replied. "I didn't realize I had taken so much time talking. Run along with Malia, Jess. Have a good time tonight. I'll meet you in my office at the cannery tomorrow morning. You'll have to take the bus in order to keep your identity a secret. Okay?"

"Okay, Dad." Jess smiled with more assurance than she felt, and her mind whirled with unanswered questions as she followed her sister to the car.

Chapter Two

When they reached the front door, Jess hesitated. "Maybe I should stay here, Malia. Dad wants to keep my real identity a secret; being seen with you might spoil his plans."

"Not this time," Malia replied. "You see, he always invites new office employees to dinner when they first go to work at Pine Pack. Then I sometimes entertain them for the evening if he's busy. It's more public relations. So you have no worries for tonight. We'll solve other problems when the time comes."

"What other problems?" Jess asked.

"Things Dad probably hasn't thought about. He has a quicksilver mind, Jess, and sometimes he talks off the top of his head. But cool logic reaches him before he makes a big mistake. Sometimes he's like two personalities wrapped in one package. For instance, he probably hasn't realized that boys are going to be asking you for dates. That means they'll be picking you up and taking you home."

"Hadn't thought of that," Jess said as she

climbed into the car. "Maybe I should rent my own apartment."

"We'll see about that later." Malia placed her violin case on the back seat of the car, slid under the wheel, and drove toward the beach.

"Where are we going?" Jess asked. "The concert hall?"

"The summer programs are held in Waikiki Shell under the stars." Malia swerved to avoid a pink and white striped jeep carrying a load of tourists. "I've brought a blanket for you to spread on the ground, and I have a pass to the grass area."

"Sounds great," Jess said. "Will you be sitting where I can see you?"

"I play first chair in the second violin section. You'll spot me eventually. There're about eighty-five orchestra members. You'll hear an outstanding concert tonight. Bertrand Baxter, the famous American pianist, will play a Beethoven concerto. The rest of the program will be from the symphonic literature of the nineteenth and twentieth centuries."

Traffic surged about them, and Jess remained silent until Malia managed to find a parking spot and eased the car into it. They walked the short distance to the orchestra shell, and Malia presented her pass, which admitted them to the grass area.

"I hear people tuning their instruments." Jess paused to listen to the muted string tones. "Are you late?"

Malia glanced at her watch. "No. The concert doesn't start until eight o'clock." She spread the blanket on the grass. "I've allowed plenty of time, but you'll have to wait a while. It's only seven-thirty. Will you mind terribly being alone?"

"Of course she'll mind," a deep voice said, "so I'll sit with her."

Jess turned toward a Polynesian man who had walked up behind them. He wore tight blue pants, sandals, and an aloha shirt hanging over the pants. His long hair curled in tendrils over his collar, touching the plumeria lei around his neck. His eyes held Jess's attention. They gleamed like polished obsidian and spoke of intelligence.

"Johnny!" Malia exclaimed. "How nice! Now I won't feel as if I'm deserting a guest. Jess, this is Johnny Kuhio. You'll be seeing a lot of him. He works in Dad's PR office — edits the house organ. Johnny, this is Jess. As of tomorrow she'll be the new girl in your office. You two get acquainted and I'll see you later. I have to run now."

"Aloha!" Johnny looked Jess over in an appraising manner. "You da kine wahine I been waiting to meet."

"What?" Jess hoped Johnny wouldn't ask her last name, which Malia had so carefully omitted in her introduction.

"You no understand de pidgin?" Johnny laughed, and Jess thought he was the most handsome young man she had ever met.

"I'm afraid not," Jess said. "Want to explain?"

"Naw." Johnny sat down on the blanket and motioned for Jess to join him. "I'll save the pidgin for the tourists at the Surfside. They expect it. So you landed a job with old man Wong."

"Mr. Wong has hired me to work in his public relations office." Jess felt guilty at her deception. She liked Johnny Kuhio, his looks, his easygoing manner, his friendliness. Surely he couldn't be the one giving away Pine Pack secrets.

"You don't look like Wong's type," Johnny said.

"And what type is that?" Jess asked.

"The money-grubbing type. I can tell by the way you're dressed that you've come from the mainland. You look like a girl who thinks for herself. Old Wong only hires yes-men — and women. He holds up dollar bills and expects them to sit up and bark the right words."

31

"If you object to the way he manages his business, why do you work there?" Jess clenched her fists. She liked this man, yet she was already at odds with him.

"I take none of his money," Johnny assured her. "I work at Pine Pack editing that paper merely to satisfy a university requirement. One copy of each issue of Pine Pack News goes into my scrapbook as proof of accomplishment. When my year is up I'll take my book and leave. But you won't be so lucky. You may be with Mr. Wong for a long time."

"I'd like to stay here forever," Jess said, trying for a light tone. "I already love the islands, and I'm sure I'll like my job."

"I'll show you the highlights of Oahu in your free hours if you'll let me. That'll take your mind off of old Wong. All he thinks about is making more money than he made the day before."

"That's unfair! If you're going to work for him, you should be loyal to him."

"I'm not working for him," Johnny pointed out. "I'm working for myself. I'm really doing him a big favor. He's getting his newspaper edited for free for a whole year. And I'm doing a good job, too."

The music began, and Jess stopped speaking and gave it her full attention. The pianist sketched a melody in black and white, then the whole orchestra joined him, its many colorful voices enlarging the sketch into a mural of sound. For a few moments Jess forgot about the prickly Johnny Kuhio. The wind swept all clouds from the star-studded sky, and she smelled the sea in the air, the sea mingled with the scent of carnations and plumeria.

As the music continued she glanced at Johnny from the corner of her eye. In repose his face showed traces of the bitterness that had flowed out in his words. Suddenly he looked directly at her, and she felt herself blushing.

"Let's go for a walk," Johnny suggested. "It's almost intermission time, and we can hear the music all up and down the beach."

"Won't we lose our place here?"

"We'll leave the blanket to mark the spot. Nobody will take it. I'll leave my shirt on it for good measure." He slipped off his aloha shirt, and his brown skin gleamed in the starlight.

Jess stood and followed Johnny from the orchestra area, and they walked toward the beach. When they reached the sand of a secluded area Johnny laughed.

"What's so funny?"

"You. Nobody tries to walk in the sand

with their shoes on."

Jess kicked off her sandals and carried them, welcoming the feel of the smooth white sand against her bare feet. They sat down on a smooth rock near the water's edge, and Jess watched the moon rise out of the sea. A coconut palm dipped its branches as if bowing a greeting.

"There's a mystery about these tropics that I love," Jess said. "Do you feel it?"

"I've felt it all my life." Johnny looked at her in admiration. "But I never expected a newcomer to notice it so soon."

"I don't feel like a newcomer. That's strange, isn't it? I guess it's because I've read so much about the islands. Tell me about your family, Johnny. I can imagine that you might be descended from the kings of old Hawaii."

"No way." Johnny laughed. "My ancestors were superior to the kings. They were kahunas, high priests. They were intellectual advisors to the kings."

"I believe you," Jess said. "You know that? I believe you."

"And why shouldn't you believe me?"

"Well, I've heard of men giving women a big line on their first date." Jess stopped, appalled that she had suggested that this casual meeting was a first date.

"I have no line," Johnny insisted. "My ancestors were kahunas. On the big island of Hawaii on the Kona Coast there is a structure called the Oracle Tower. There was once a temple there dedicated to the great god Kane. That is where some of my ancestors worshipped and received their wisdom. Today I receive mine from the university."

"A much more practical arrangement, I'd say." Jess smiled.

"Practical for whom?" Johnny asked. "My friends and I are planning a revolution. We'd like to see Hawaii go back to the old ways, the ways before the wonderful missionaries came here to educate the natives."

"I think it's impossible for a country to go backward." Jess sifted sand between her fingers. "Everything moves forward. Progress, you know."

"These islands are nothing but tourist traps today. That's why I'm getting the best education I can manage. Foreigners have come here and taken over. They've put the true Polynesians down. We're supposed to be satisfied with a guitar, a surfboard, and a pretty girl. It really isn't such a bad arrangement, but I'd like it a great deal more if the foreigners didn't also expect us Polynesians to be the flunkies of the islands, the baggage boys, the beach boys, the tour guides."

"This is America," Jess said. "You can be whatever you want to be. If you're a beach boy, it's of your own choosing."

"I work as a beach boy to earn just enough for food and shelter. When I finish my education, I'll educate others. Someday there'll be a quiet revolution. Or maybe a not-so-quiet revolution. When it's over, Hawaii will be the island paradise it was before the whalers and missionaries arrived."

"You're a dreamer." Jess laughed. Something about Johnny Kuhio repelled her at the same time it attracted her. It was as if he were two different people at the same time, the simple beach boy and the revolutionary scholar.

"Maybe I'm a dreamer, but I'm a practical dreamer," Johnny said. "It's time man considered the quality in living, the why instead of the how much. Man is going to have to look within himself for answers. Only as he sees a greater quality in life than material possessions can he begin to understand the greater quality within himself."

"That sounds like a good philosophy," Jess said. "But you're overlooking human nature. History has proved that it's the profit motive that stirs individuals to productivity. Over and over again men are judged by their ability to produce."

"What about wars?" Johnny asked. "Then they're praised for their ability to destroy. Foreigners have made a war of sorts on my islands."

"I'm sure I don't have all the answers," Jess said. "I just don't think any people can go back to the 'old ways' of living. It's impossible."

"I want to show you something." Johnny eased from the rock where he had been seated, jogged to an ekoa thicket, and pulled a surfboard from hiding. He dragged it back to where Jess sat.

"Whose is it?" Jess asked.

"Mine. This is a special spot I come to whenever I get too fed up with the establishment. I'm going to show you a bit of old Hawaii." In an instant Johnny skinned from his blue pants and stood before her clad only in brief swimming trunks. He dropped his plumeria lei into her lap, then he splashed into the surf. Jess watched the moonlight gleam on his bronze body. Pushing the board in front of him, he swam out to where the big breakers were forming.

Jess gasped when he disappeared from view for a moment. What if he had had an accident? Where would she go for help? But Johnny Kuhio was in no trouble. Moments later Jess saw him standing on the surf-board, his pencil-slim body silhouetted against the sky. Gracefully he balanced himself on the board as it skimmed across the water, and Jess felt her scalp tingle. The old Hawaii. For these few moments Johnny Kuhio had turned back the clock. Jess felt as if she were watching a scene from ancient days.

When the wave smashed onto the sand, Johnny leaped from his board, grabbed it, and ran upon the beach where Jess waited.

"That's how it used to be!" he exclaimed. "A man rode the waves when he wanted pleasure. He ate when he was hungry, and he slept when he was tired. Those days could come again, Jess. If enough people wanted them, they would come again."

"It's a dream, Johnny. A beautiful dream, perhaps, but nonetheless a dream."

"How about dreaming with me to-morrow?" Johnny asked. "I'll teach you how to ride the waves."

"I'm not very good at water sports," Jess said.

"I said I'd teach you. How about it? What time do you get off work?"

"Around five o'clock, I suppose."

"Good. I'll meet you then. We'll go to the Surfside and change into swimsuits in their beach house, then we'll come here. Is it a date?"

Jess nodded. "It's a date. I'll look forward to it. But right now we'd better get back to the concert."

Johnny slipped into his blue pants, and Jess dropped his plumeria lei around his neck.

"You forgot something," Johnny reminded.

Jess kissed the tip of her forefinger, then placed it gently on Johnny's lips. When they left the sand beach, they slipped back into their sandals, and when they reached Malia's blanket, in the grass area, the concert was just ending.

"I'd like to take you home," Johnny said.

"Let's make it another time. I came with Malia, and I'd better leave with her."

"Got to impress her old man, I suppose," Johnny agreed. "But I'll see you tomorrow. Remember."

"I'll remember." Jess smiled as Johnny disappeared into the crowd. Several minutes passed before Malia returned, but Jess wasn't bored. Johnny Kuhio filled her mind, and the crowd that surged around her filled her eyes and ears.

"Johnny desert you?" Malia asked, arriving with violin case in hand.

39

"He had to go, but we had a great evening. I'll have to admit that we didn't hear all of the concert, though. Did you know that he's great on a surfboard?"

"I know." Malia laughed. "That's his job at the Surfside Hotel. He teaches the guests to ride the board. He's a smooth operator, Jess. Don't get carried away."

As they walked toward the car Jess told Malia of her plans for the next evening. "It's all right to go out with him, isn't it?"

"Of course," Malia said. "Just don't get carried away. He's a heartbreaker in spite of his strange back-to-the-old-days ideas."

Malia chatted all the way back to the house, then she grew quiet as they entered the front door.

"Dad always goes to bed early so he can get up early," she explained. "But he won't hear us over on our wing of the house. Let's get ready for bed, then talk for a while, okay?"

"Okay."

Jess showered and slipped into a comfortable robe. It seemed that she had been up for about twenty-six hours. She hadn't realized how tired she was. She stretched out on the bed, and she was almost in a doze when Malia tapped on her door and peeked inside.

"Oh, you're tired," Malia said. "We can talk later."

"No, come on in," Jess invited. "I have a slight problem to solve and I need to talk to you. I told you that Johnny asked me for a surfing date. He'll pick me up at the office, but where shall I have him bring me home?"

"I've been thinking about that," Malia said. "Ora has a sister who works about three blocks from here. And her family has gone for a vacation on the mainland. I'll give you the address, and you can have Johnny take you there. I'll arrange it with Ora's sister."

"Thanks, Malia. I really dislike sneaking around, but if it'll help Dad . . ."

"He thinks it will," Malia said. "It may be just another of his wild schemes, but they pass. Humor him for a while at least. Frankly, I'm dying to tell the world you're my sister. It's going to be hard to keep it a secret. What is your mother like?"

Jess stared at the floor.

"If you'd rather not tell me, I'll understand. It's just that I find it strange to think that we have the same father but different mothers. My mother was from a Polynesian family on Maui. She was small and dark and beautiful, and she played the piano. That's her instrument in my studio."

"Dad's had a sad life, hasn't he?" Jess asked. "I mean his first marriage flopped, and then he lost his second wife. I didn't know that until now."

"I guess that's why he throws himself so totally into his work."

"My mother is very tall and very blond," Jess said. "Her parents came to America from Germany, and she lives near them in New York. That's where I grew up. It's a great city, but not as beautiful as Honolulu. I asked mother once why she left the islands."

"What did she say?"

"It happened after the Pearl Harbor attack," Jess said. "Lots of people fled to the mainland. Mother flew back to New York, but Dad stayed here."

"Lots of Chinese stayed." Malia nodded. "They bought up land, and later it made them wealthy."

"After the war ended Dad came to New York and lived with Mother for a few years. But she had changed. Dad hadn't bargained for a successful artist as a wife."

"It made that much difference?" Malia asked.

"I guess it did. Mother had made a name for herself, locally at least. She felt there

42

was nothing for her in Hawaii, and Dad knew there was nothing for him in New York. So they were divorced." Jess sighed. "I know the reasons, but sometimes I still can't understand them. Over the years Mother has become an outstanding American artist. I suppose I can't blame her for refusing to give up being a person in her own right."

"Maybe there are some things a person has to accept without understanding," Malia said. "I know Dad is totally devoted to the islands. He has told me about the war years when many mainlanders got scared and headed for home. I've always admired him for staying. He bought up the land the haoles vacated, and he built his canning empire. But I'm boring you. Get some sleep. I'll see you tomorrow."

Before Jess could protest, Malia had glided from the room and closed the door. Jess opened the sliding glass partitions onto her lanai and gazed up at the stars. Malia's questions had probed at old wounds. But she was an adult now; she would forget the childish hurt growing up in a broken home had caused. She would only remember her vow to make marriage a forever thing if the right man ever came her way.

As Jess climbed into bed she shivered,

thinking about her new job. How could she face Johnny Kuhio in an office situation? How could she suspect him of deceit and at the same time plan to go surfing with him at five o'clock?

Chapter Three

Jess slept fitfully that night, and the next morning after she had been awake for a few minutes she knew what she had to do. While dressing carefully but simply in a blue tailored skirt and blouse, she planned what she would say to her father. Ten minutes later at the breakfast table she waited for her chance to say it. Her sister had not joined them yet, and her father was scanning the headlines in the morning paper.

Today Ora flitted between kitchen and dining table in a mint-green uniform, her bracelets ajangle. She served papaya halves garnished with small lavender orchids, buttered toast swimming in coconut syrup, and coffee. The exotic food fascinated Jess, and she had to force herself to keep her mind on business.

"Dad?"

Her father looked up from the paper, and although Jess sensed that she didn't have his full attention, she continued speaking. She was beginning to realize that her father could keep on top of several situations at the same time.

"Dad, last night I balked when you asked me to change my name, then I calmed down and agreed. But I've been thinking it over since then, and I have some questions."

"Let's hear them." Mr. Wong stirred his coffee, although he had added no sugar to it.

"Under the circumstances I don't see how I can live here even if I use a different name. People would be almost as suspicious of your house guest as of your daughter, wouldn't they?"

"I suppose that's right," her father said, thoughtfully creasing the newspaper. "But who'll know that you're living here?"

"That's another problem. Last night I met Johnny Kuhio. I agreed to go out with him late this afternoon. After our date I can hardly ask him to take me back to the cannery."

Her father frowned. "We do have a problem. I hadn't thought of that."

"And what about this morning?" Jess continued. "Surely I'll have to fill out personnel forms. When I write my address, won't your staff recognize it as yours?"

"They might at that." Mr. Wong drummed his fingers on the tabletop. "Guess I didn't think this plan through very carefully, Jess."

"It would work out all right if I lived in an apartment of my own. I'll do that if you want me to."

"Of course I won't have that. I want you here, and so does Malia. Perhaps you'd better just appear as Jess Wong. But I still want you to keep your eyes and ears open in the PR office. Okay?"

"Okay, Dad. And I think this way will be better. If I went by another name, someone would find out the truth sooner or later. Then there would be explaining to do. Your employees might resent the deception. Bad public relations, no?"

"Bad public relations, yes." Mr. Wong laughed as he pushed his chair from the table. "If you'll excuse me, I have some small chores to do before we go to work."

Jess sighed in relief. Standing up to her father hadn't been as bad as she had expected. Malia still hadn't appeared for breakfast, and Ora was in the kitchen. Jess welcomed being alone for a few minutes. Now she knew her father a bit better than she had yesterday, and she liked what she knew. He might represent big business, but Johnny Kuhio was dead wrong about him. He didn't always insist on being yessed; he could change his mind, and change it quickly if a situation warranted it. Jess suspected that her father had many hidden facets to his personality.

Later, as she and her dad rode along the palm-lined streets toward the cannery, Jess clutched her purse and her beach bag nervously as she expressed her growing self doubts.

"I hope I can handle this job, Dad. I'd hate to disappoint you — and myself."

"I think you'll do fine once you've had some experience." Mr. Wong honked at the car ahead of him an instant after the traffic light turned green. "You've proved to me this morning that you think clearly. Can you type?"

"Yes. I suppose that's an essential."

"Right. There's usually some typing involved. But what's more important, PR people are image builders. Reeta and Alex will insist on clear, concise writing, and there'll probably be times when they'll expect you to work under pressure. You can learn a lot from Alex. He senses the news aspect of a situation and knows exactly what to do about it. I'd hate to lose him."

"Is that a danger?"

"He's due for a step up. I may promote him to head of the advertising department. But that's top secret. Don't breathe a word."

Jess nodded.

"Over the years your letters have told me that you're a creative person, Jess. I hope you'll like working ideas into practical programs. And I hope you'll be sensitive to people — aware of their moods and responses. When you're puzzled over any situation, always ask yourself what results you want. The answer should be goodwill."

Jess had no more time for qualms and misgivings. She inhaled the sweet scent of fresh pineapple as Mr. Wong parked his car in a reserved slot bearing his name. Together they walked toward Pine Pack. The main office squatted on the street level, but other cannery buildings had been terraced into the hillside that rose behind the parking lot.

"What a beautiful building!" Jess paused outside the office doorway and touched the dark, rough-textured wall. "What kind of rock is this?"

"The main construction is of concrete, but it's hidden by this lava rock facade. That dresses the office up quite a bit."

Inside the building Jess gazed at plastic skylights and countless windows and sliding doors.

Following her gaze her father said, "We try to catch the tradewinds whenever possible." He led the way down a hallway to the personnel office, standing aside to let Jess enter first.

A thin reed of a woman stepped forward and greeted them.

"Miss Laclede, this is my daughter, Jess Wong. I've already decided that she'll work in the PR office, but I want her to fill out the necessary forms and questionnaires."

"Yes, sir." Miss Laclede nodded to her boss, then turned to Jess. "I'm happy to know you, Miss Wong. Please sit down at that desk by the window, and I'll be right with you."

Mr. Wong smilingly paused as he started to leave the office. "I'll return in a few minutes and take you on a tour of the cannery, Jess."

Jess felt like a statue on exhibition; news traveled quickly at Pine Pack. Many people stopped in the personnel office on errands, and Jess felt their eyes scrutinizing her, studying the boss's new daughter. But she took her time filling out the forms, and before she finished, her father returned.

"I suppose you felt as if you were passing in review," he said when they were alone in the hallway once more.

Jess grinned. "There were quite a few people in and out."

"I've always kept your picture on my

desk, and now everyone's eager to see you in person. Here. Let's stop at your home base first." Mr. Wong paused in front of a door with a frosted glass window bearing the words Public Relations Office. Opening the door, he let Jess step ahead of him, then he guided her toward a handsome Oriental man sitting behind the largest desk in the office.

"Jess, I'd like you to meet your boss, Alex Yanagisako. Alex, this is my daughter, Jess."

"How do you do, Mr. Yanagisako." Jess shook the well-manicured hand that extended from the sleeve of Mr. Yanagisako's expensively tailored sportcoat. "I'm looking forward to working with you."

"It will be my pleasure," Alex Yanagisako replied. "Come with me and I'll introduce you to your co-workers."

"Make it quick, Alex," Jess's father said. "I want to show Jess through the cannery this morning."

"Yes, sir." Alex nodded, and as he led the way toward a smaller desk where a slim, blonde-haired girl sat typing, Jess noticed that he was just a trifle shorter than she. His dark hair and eyes matched his silk slacks, and he reminded Jess of a porpoise, sleek and slim and full of charm and friendly curiosity.

"Jess Wong, I'd like you to know Reeta McQuigg. Reeta, this is Rick Wong's daughter from the mainland."

Jess started to offer her hand in greeting, but Reeta made no such motion; so Jess dropped her arm to her side. Reeta McQuigg was like a Dresden figurine or a sculpture molded in snow. Everything about her was white. Her hair was platinum blonde, her complexion was creamy, and she wore a white dress and white pumps. Her amber eyes sparked two circles of color on her face, giving her a catlike quality. Jess found herself listening for Reeta to purr.

"Glad you're to work with us," Reeta said. "I have some jobs ready and waiting for you."

"They'll have to wait a bit longer," Alex said. "Mr. Wong will show Jess through the cannery this morning. Come over to this next desk, Jess and meet Johnny Kuhio."

For an instant Jess froze. How was Johnny going to take the news that she was his boss's daughter? She caught a glimpse of her father still standing in the doorway, and she hoped Johnny wouldn't make a scene.

"Miss Wong and I have already met." Johnny rose in his slow, easygoing manner and towered above her and Alex, his face impassive.

"Good," Alex said. "Now that you've met us all, Jess, you're free to go on tour with your father. I'll be looking for you back here this afternoon."

"Thank you." Jess joined her father at the door, and once they were in the hallway she sighed.

"Was that such an ordeal?" he asked.

"Not at all," Jess said. "It's just that they all seem to be waiting for me, expecting so much from me."

"Naturally they expect their own work loads to be lightened. You can hardly blame them for that."

"Such a racial mixture!" Jess exclaimed. "Chinese, Japanese, Polynesian. Are you ever troubled with racial tensions?"

"Hardly ever," her father said. "We're all Hawaiians, no matter what else our ancestry may hold."

Jess followed her father through a heavy door that separated the offices from the stairway that led up to the cannery proper. Here, in a large shell of a building, noise assailed her from all sides, and the fragrance of pineapple hung sharp and sweet all about. The sound of running water all but drowned out her father's words.

"Kelli Puno is in charge of the machinery that cleans the fruit when it comes off the trucks." Mr. Wong waved at Kelli, who returned the greeting and continued with his work. He was short and squat, and his face was so plump that his eyes almost disappeared when he smiled. Jess thought that he looked a lot like a pineapple himself.

"Then here's the Ginaca machine that removes the inedible portions of the fruit and converts it into the desired form. See the cored cylinders on that conveyor belt?"

Jess nodded.

"Each fruit cylinder is inspected to make sure it is free from blemishes. Fred and Ned Kapalana are our inspectors, and that's Perry Lee you see managing the automatic slicing machine. Lou Turner operates the filling machine."

Jess wondered if her father expected her to remember all the names he was reeling off. Surely there must be a roster of employees somewhere. She watched as the open cans were mechanically conveyed from the filling machine to the sealing machine.

"Once the cans are sealed they are heat processed, then cooled. Later they are labeled by machines."

"This is all sliced pineapple," Jess said. "Do you also can crushed fruit and juice?"

Her father nodded, and together they visited other sections of the cannery including the special rooms where frozen fruit was processed. When they were finished, Jess sighed.

"And to think that I have always taken pineapple for granted!"

"That's exactly what we want our customers to do," her father replied. "We do the work for the customer's pleasure and enjoyment. But right now, it's time for lunch."

Jess felt hungry, but she knew that she wouldn't be able to eat much. She was too excited. How would she ever face the three in public relations who seemed to expect so much from her? What if she bombed out on her first job that really counted?

Chapter Four

By the time Jess returned to the public relations office, Johnny Kuhio had left for his other job at the Surfside Hotel. She sighed in relief. Johnny attracted her, and she doubted that she would have been able to keep her mind on her work if he had been around. Was he furious with her for not telling him she was Rick Wong's daughter? What if he stood her up tonight? Jess tried to put the questions from her mind as she listened to Alex Yanagisako brief her on her new duties.

"This will be your desk." Alex smiled and patted the top of the smallest desk in the office, which was directly in front of the one Reeta McQuigg occupied. "I have some material that I want you to read, brochures and reports that will familiarize you with the inner workings of Pine Pack." Her boss plunked a manila folder on her desk, opened it, and fanned a group of pamphlets into view.

"Thank you, Mr. Yanagisako, I'll start reading right away."

"And call me Alex. We're very informal

here in PR. I'll be out for an hour or two, but Reeta will be here in case you need anything or have any questions."

Jess smiled, and as she began thumbing through the brochures she felt a bit more at ease. She scanned an organization chart, an annual report, and several recent newspaper clippings. But a copy of the company's history held her full attention, and she began reading it thoroughly and carefully. She was about halfway through it when Reeta McQuigg stopped at her desk.

"The galleys for the next issue of *Pine Pack News* just arrived, Jess. I wish you'd proof them for me before you leave this afternoon. The copy has been edited; all you have to do is to mark the typographical errors with this green ballpoint." Reeta laid the galleys and the pen on Jess's desk.

Jess shoved her pamphlets aside, but before she could speak Reeta said, "You can take that other stuff home with you and read it tonight. It's just background material. I'm going to the ladies' room to wash my hands. Be back in a few minutes." Reeta held her hands away from her body as if they were filthy, but Jess saw nothing on them.

After Reeta left, Jess studied the galleys. So this was Johnny Kuhio's house organ. She thumbed through all eight pages, then she started reading on page one, marking errors as she went. It was almost three o'clock when Alex strode into the office, his hands full of photographs and manila envelopes.

"Through reading already?" Alex paused by Jess's desk.

"Hardly," Jess replied. "Reeta asked me to proofread these galleys, but I'll get back to the brochures soon."

Alex frowned slightly, but before he could comment Reeta joined them. "I asked her to work for me today, Alex. I'm behind, and publication date is rushing toward us."

"I've finished proofing," Jess said. "What an interesting paper! I had no idea that a business publication could be so thought-provoking."

"Just put the copy in my in basket," Reeta said. "Then you can go to the machine at the end of the hall and bring us all some coffee. We're due for a fifteen-minute break." Reeta tapped the toe of her white pump against the floor, and Jess felt her impatience. Was this what her father had meant by working under pressure?

"You'll find some change in the petty-cash drawer in my desk," Reeta said. "Top drawer on the left."

Jess walked to Reeta's desk, dropped the

galleys in the in basket, and took some coins from the cash drawer. As she started to leave the room Alex and Reeta were deeply engrossed in the glossy prints Alex had spread out on his desk.

"Cream or sugar?" Jess asked.

For a moment neither Reeta nor Alex answered her, and Jess felt like an intruder. Then Reeta sighed, batted her eyes at Alex, and said, as if speaking to a child, "We both take it black."

Possessiveness rang in Reeta's "we," and she stood so close to Alex that her hair brushed against his hand as she leaned over the pictures. Jess left the office quietly. She had to wait for three people in line at the coffee machine, and she had filled only two cups when Alex called to her.

"Hold it, Jess. We'll take Reeta's coffee to her when we go back to the office. Let's take our break out on the lanai."

"Is that allowed?" Jess asked.

"Definitely." Alex smiled and led the way outdoors. "That's why Mr. Wong had it built. He believes that everyone works more efficiently if they take regular breaks in a pleasant place." Alex took the coffee from Jess and set it on a round table shaded by a candy-striped umbrella. Similar tables ringed a small pool where a pineapple-shaped fountain splashed water into a bed of yellow and white water lilies.

"How beautiful!" Jess exclaimed. "Sometimes I can hardly believe that all this is real. I'm afraid I'll wake up and find myself back in New York waiting tables in the Tic-Tock Cafe."

"Is that what you did before you came here?" Alex made no pretense at hiding his curiosity.

Jess nodded. "I've earned a teaching degree, but no jobs were available, so Dad invited me here."

"You may find that you like public relations." Alex leaned forward in his chair. "At least I hope so. You're a welcome addition to the office."

Jess lowered her eyes to avoid Alex's penetrating gaze. Was there a double meaning in his words?

"If you stick with PR you'll find that you can make a good living." Alex ran his hand over his sleek black hair. "You may begin at about seven thousand a year, but the sky's the limit. You might wind up as PR director for a major corporation at a fantastic salary."

"How long have you been with Pine Pack?" Jess recalled her father's words about a promotion for Alex.

"A little over ten years," Alex said. "I started here fresh out of high school, but I've almost earned a business degree from the university by enrolling in night classes."

"Do you have bigger jobs in mind, or is that an unfair question?"

"I plan to stick with Pine Pack as long as Rick Wong runs it. He's a great guy."

"I really don't know him very well, but I like what I've seen so far." Jess glanced at her watch. "Alex! We've already overstayed our coffee break. Where did the minutes go?"

Alex grinned impishly. "That's what the girls always say when they're out with Alex Yanagisako. If you'd like to continue our discussion, I'd love to take you to dinner."

Jess felt herself flush with pleasure. "I'm sorry, but I've made other plans for tonight. Thank you just the same."

"Maybe we can make it another time; but right now we'd better get back to PR. And we'd better have a cup of coffee for Reeta."

Jess stood, trying to hide her reluctance to leave. Back inside, they paused at the coffee machine while Alex filled a cup for Reeta. When they entered the PR office, Reeta glanced pointedly at her watch, but she merely murmured a thank you when Alex gave her the coffee.

Jess resumed her reading of the company brochures, but when Alex left the room on another errand, Reeta walked to her desk and tapped her toe until Jess looked up.

"Here's a sales report that might interest you." She dropped the paper onto Jess's desk.

"Thank you." Jess picked up the report and added it to her sheaf of unread material.

"Enjoy your coffee break with Alex the Amorous?" Reeta's amber eyes flashed like caution signals.

Inwardly Jess flinched at Reeta's caustic tone, but she smiled. "Yes, he's an interesting person."

"Interesting!" Reeta snorted. "Let me warn you. He gives all the new girls the big rush, then he drops them like a ship drops anchor. You're the new girl now. Your little sister is about to get the business from Alex, but she's too dumb to know it."

"Do you speak from experience?" Jess couldn't resist the question.

"Of course not." Reeta flipped her blonde mane over her shoulders. "I wouldn't date a Japanese."

"That's strange. You seem content to work for a Chinese." Jess snapped the words before she remembered that she was speaking to her business superior.

"My work and my private life are two entirely different areas." Reeta pulled a white tissue from her pocket and wiped her fingers on it. "You have a lot to learn about Hawaii. Socially, the ethnic groups tend to segregate themselves; of course, everyone is equal in the business world. But if you're going to carry a surfboard-size chip on your shoulder, I'm perfectly willing to let you find these things out for yourself."

"I'm sorry I snapped at you, Reeta. I've an infuriating habit of speaking before my mind edits my thoughts."

"I understand," Reeta said. "I'm sure we'll get along okay. The McQuiggs have always known how to manage people."

"The McQuiggs? Do other members of your family work here?"

"No." Reeta shook her head. "What I meant was that my ancestors were aboard the first ship that brought missionaries to Lahaina over a hundred years ago. The McQuiggs have always known how to get along with the natives. If we hadn't taught the Polynesians our ways, they'd still be lazy pagans. And if we hadn't brought in the Japanese and the Chinese to work the cane fields, the islands would be poverty stricken."

Jess smiled, although Reeta's conversation grated like a fingernail against slate. "How can you and Johnny Kuhio stand to work in the same office?"

"Why do you ask that?" Reeta wiped her hands down the sides of her white dress. "What do you know about Johnny Kuhio? You only met him this morning. Didn't you?"

Jess ignored the question and tried to return to her reading, but Reeta kept talking.

"I suppose you're going to be like all the other girls," she said. "They fall for Johnny Kuhio before they ever hear him say a word in that disgusting pidgin he insists on using."

At that moment Alex strode back into the office, and Reeta returned to her own desk. Jess couldn't keep her mind on the material assigned to her, but she forced her eyes on it and pretended to be reading. Reeta's low opinion of both Johnny and Alex bothered her. Was there truth in her words? Or was she just cutting her co-workers down in an effort to build up her own self-esteem? And did Malia date Alex?

Jess could imagine that the girls might go for Johnny Kuhio, but she had a harder time believing that Alex was a chaser. He had been friendly. He had asked her for a date.

But he certainly hadn't pressed his attentions on her against her will. She wondered who Reeta McQuigg dated. And if she was so down on Alex, why did she bat her long lashes at him? Why did she . . .

"Miss Wong?" Reeta broke into Jess's thoughts as she swished up to her desk once more. "You'll have to rework these galleys. Accuracy is the watchword of the public relations office, and you've done a careless job of proofing."

"What's the trouble?" Alex strode to Jess's desk and took the galleys from Reeta's hands.

"I found ten misspelled words in the first five pages," Reeta said. "The green marks are Jess's. The red ones are mine. She'll have to reproof the whole thing."

"Did you give Jess a roster of names to use for checking spelling?" Alex asked. "All these errors are in proper names — names unfamiliar to a mainlander."

Reeta took the galleys and scrutinized them, then she looked up at Alex as if he had just discovered a new continent. "Why of course you're right, Alex. I have a roster right on my desk." Reeta's heels clicked as she walked to her desk to get the list.

"I'm sorry, Alex," Jess said. "I should have had enough sense to ask for a roster. I shouldn't have taken it for granted that the names were spelled properly. It's just as easy to make a typo on a name as on any other word."

"You're right there," Alex agreed. "And next time you'll know you should check. A person's name is dear to him, and he hates to see it misspelled. That's important to know in any writing that you may do for us. But it's doubly important when it comes to the house organ, the *Pine Pack News*. This is a paper for insiders — for the employees of Pine Pack. We mail it to their homes so the whole family can read it. We try to mention as many names as possible; seeing his name gives an employee a sense of importance, of belonging."

"I'll check each name carefully," Jess promised. "I'm sorry I goofed."

"It won't be the last time," Alex said. "It takes a while to catch on to the ins and outs of this business. This was basically Reeta's error for withholding proper instructions. In all fairness, she should be the one to reread the galleys, but it's more practical to let you do it. You're going to have to become familiar with our employees' names, and this is an excellent way to begin. Gradually you'll begin to associate names with faces, and each step of this learning process makes you a more valuable employee."

Reeta returned with the roster and plunked it onto Jess's desk without a word.

"Thank you, Reeta. I'll finish the proofing before I leave the office tonight."

"Good," Reeta said.

"No need to work overtime, Jess." Alex scowled at Reeta. "There's no big rush at this point. If you're through by tomorrow noon, all will be on schedule."

Jess smiled at Alex, but even as she smiled she wondered how she was going to manage in this office. Both Alex and Reeta were her superiors and she wanted to please them, but there was a friction between them that she didn't understand.

"Don't look so puzzled." Alex laughed. "Things will get worse before they get better. There'll be days when you'll leave ten or a dozen things unfinished at quitting time. I might as well show you right now how to make out a daily schedule, a checklist."

Alex hurried across the office to a file cabinet, then returned to Jess's desk with a calendar pad. "Keep this on your desk at all times. Before you leave the office each night, jot down the things to be done the next day in order of their importance. I'll do it for you this time."

Alex leaned over Jess's desk and wrote:

67

Finish proofing house organ. Finish reading company brochures.

"There." He placed the calendar on her desk so that it was exactly in line with the edge of her blotter. "That'll get you off to an efficient start tomorrow morning. We'll work from there. It's five o'clock. Quitting time."

"Thanks, Alex." Jess sighed. "It's been quite a day."

Jess made a show of putting papers in drawers, trying to stall until Reeta and Alex left the room, but they both seemed to be waiting for her. At last there was nothing more she could do, so she smiled at them and picked up her purse and her beach bag.

"Good evening. I'll see you in the morning."

Jess left the office and hurried down the hallway and out the front door. Johnny Kuhio was lounging against a palm tree near the parking lot, and Jess hurried toward him. Today he wore tight red pants and a white busboy's jacket, which hung open to the waist. An orchid blossom perched jauntily behind one ear. He reached out and took Jess's hand as she reached him, and his touch warmed her until she felt Reeta's icy stare as she passed them on the way to her car.

Chapter Five

Jess withdrew her hand from Johnny's, feeling like a guilt-ridden child caught stealing cookies. What ailed her? She usually got along well with people, yet she felt a hearty dislike for Reeta McQuigg. And she knew she must remain neutral — at least until she and her dad learned who was peddling Pine Pack secrets to their competitors. But how could she feel neutral! Alex. Reeta. Johnny. None of them inspired neutral feelings.

"Rough day?" Johnny grinned and his voice flowed with a liquid softness.

"Everything's so new," Jess said. "And I made a mess of some proofreading Reeta assigned me."

"A mess in whose opinion?" Johnny headed toward the Surfside Hotel.

"In everyone's opinion. I let a bunch of misspelled names slip by me, but Reeta caught them in time."

"That figures." Johnny scowled. "I suppose she forgot to give you a roster."

Jess nodded. "I should have asked for one."

"Don't let Miss Missionary bother you. Sometimes I think the only way she can look good is to make someone else look bad. But Alex knows her tricks. He'll treat you right."

Jess thought of Alex and their coffee break. Was Johnny being serious or sarcastic?

"Let's forget about Pine Pack and public relations until tomorrow," Jess said. "Right now I'm ready for a good time. What're we going to do?"

"They say the best things in life are free, so I thought we'd go surfing as we had planned." Johnny glanced at the beach bag in Jess's hand. "I see you brought your swimsuit."

It was only a short walk to the hotel, but when they arrived on the grounds they had to slow down. A throng of children milled around the beach area.

"Look!" Jess pointed. "Someone's giving away balloons. Helium balloons!"

"The hotel does this once a week." Johnny laughed. "The Surfside has a public relations director, too."

They threaded their way through the shouting children, then Johnny directed Jess to a dressing cubicle and sat down in the sand to wait for her. The dressing room was really nothing more than a wood-fenced square of sand. Jess glanced up at blue sky bisected by a plumeria branch. Pink petals dropped around her as she changed into her swimsuit and beach robe and slipped her feet into rubber thongs.

Emerging from the dressing room, Jess looked around for Johnny, but he was nowhere in sight. She leaned against a palm tree and watched the children playing. As she waited, one small girl released her balloon and it floated toward the clouds.

"That's too bad," Jess said. "Maybe you can get another one."

"I really don't want another one." The girl grinned. "I like to see balloons float away and disappear into the sky. I'm going to watch this one as long as I can, then I'm going to make up a story about where it went."

"Will you tell the story to us?" asked a little boy standing nearby. He shaded his eyes with his hand and gazed after the ascending balloon.

"I may even write the story down," the girl said. "If it's good enough, I may write it down."

"Will you let us read it?" another girl asked. "I liked the one you wrote about the falling star."

"I'll tell you later," the first girl replied,

then she lay down on the sand and followed the balloon with her eyes and her dreams.

"She lose her balloon?" Johnny asked, joining Jess who stood in the crowd of children that had gathered around the girl.

"Don't worry about her," Jess said. "I think she lost a balloon and found something much more precious."

"Enough balloons and kids," Johnny said. "Let's go see if the surf's up."

Jess fell into step beside Johnny, and they strolled along in comfortable silence. Traffic sped by in the street near the beach. Laughing couples dashed through the sand. But Jess felt as if she and Johnny were alone. He seemed to draw a circle around them that shut out intruders.

When they reached Johnny's special cove, they found it deserted.

"Why doesn't anyone come here?" Jess asked. "It's such a beautiful spot!"

Johnny grinned. "Part of my beach boy job is to warn the hotel guests of dangerous tides or undesirable water. I paint a dim picture of this place, and the tourists take me at my word. So here we have our private cove."

Jess dropped her beach bag onto the sand, but Johnny picked it up and placed it on a rock. "The tide. Always play it safe and stash your gear up high."

Johnny grinned as he strolled to the secret spot where he kept his surfboard hidden. He pulled it onto the sand and carried it into the shallows.

"Come on, Jess. Hang onto the side and I'll paddle us out to the reef. We'll catch a big wave and ride it back to shore."

Jess splashed into the water behind Johnny, tasting the salt spray on her lips as she grabbed hold of the board. The water felt cold and smooth against her warm skin, and the surging motion of the sea exhilarated her. They eased toward the reef.

"Are there sharks around here?" Jess felt her heart pounding almost as hard as the surf as they eased toward the reef.

"No sharks." Johnny smiled down at her. "You wouldn't catch me out here if there were."

When at last they reached the watery destination Johnny had in mind, he helped Jess onto the surfboard, then he stood behind her, his bronze wet body gleaming in the sunlight.

"Can you stand up?" he asked as she peered over her shoulder at him.

"Do I have to?" Jess eyed the swirling bottle-green water. "I'm a fair lake swimmer — Red Cross lessons and all that

— but I've never had any experience in the ocean."

"But I have." Johnny winked. "Trust me. It'll be more fun if you stand up."

Jess was about to refuse when Johnny's muscled arms came around her from behind, pulling her upright. Somehow she managed to force herself to her feet as the wave swept them toward shore. Strangely enough she wasn't afraid. Johnny's body was like solid lava, and in those moments she trusted him completely. He was firm as a rock, a Polynesian god in command of his universe.

Jess blinked as the sea spray blinded her.

"Tilt your chin high into the wind," Johnny shouted in her ear as they skimmed across the reef. "That'll break the force of wind and water."

Jess obeyed, and in moments she could see again, see the thundering surf at her feet and Diamond Head jutting out from the distant shore. For many moments the comber maintained its rush toward the sand, but in the next instant Jess saw the surf break and she felt the board sink into the ebbing waves. She jumped from the board just before her head went under water, but Johnny managed to stand in the shifting sand and hold the board from floating to sea on the outgoing waves.

"That was great!" Jess laughed after she caught her breath. "I had no idea surfing could be such a thrill."

"Want to go out again?"

"Thanks, but I've had enough for the first time. You go again if you want to. I'll wait here."

With one fluid movement Johnny turned the board, pointing it back toward the reef. Without her weight dragging on the side Johnny skimmed through the sea to his favorite spot. Jess watched as he let three waves come in, then caught the fourth one. Again Johnny reminded her of a god walking across the water, and for a moment she saw a flashing glimpse of the old Hawaii — the Hawaii Johnny wished to restore to the twentieth century.

This time when the surf broke, Johnny submerged, but he surfaced clinging to his board.

"Do you come here often?" Jess asked after Johnny put his surfboard back into its hiding place.

"Not often enough. I could spend all day riding those waves and never be bored. Are you hungry?"

Jess nodded. "But I hate to leave here. This cove is peaceful as a cathedral."

"Who said anything about leaving?"

Johnny pulled a packet of hard rolls, a wedge of cheese, and a bottle of wine from his beach bag. "Compliments of the Surfside." Taking a small knife from the packet, he sliced the bread and cheese.

"I've never tasted a better meal," Jess said.

"You're probably missing steak smothered with mushrooms by not eating on the elegant Wong lanai," Johnny said. "Why didn't you tell me you were Rick Wong's daughter?"

"You didn't ask." Jess smiled and bit off some cheese. "But I'm sorry I wasn't honest with you, and I'm glad you're not angry."

They ate in silence for a few minutes, then Johnny asked, "What gave you the idea of coming to Honolulu to work in public relations?"

"My dad," Jess answered. "I wanted to teach school, elementary grades, but there just aren't any jobs open. I worked for a year as a waitress in a fancy restaurant thinking something would open up this summer. But nothing did. So when Dad invited me here, I leaped at the chance to come."

"And you gave up your teaching ambition just like that?" Johnny snapped his fingers.

Jess glanced sharply at Johnny when she heard his critical tone. "What would you

76

have me do? Spend my whole life as a wait-ress?"

"We have schools here, you know. Have you applied at any of them?"

"No. I didn't even think about such a possibility. Dad said he needed me at Pine Pack, and that was that."

"You just can't give up teaching that easily." Johnny leaned toward her almost upsetting the wine. "You're indebted. Think of all the teachers who have helped you. You have an obligation to pass that help on to someone else. And many people need it. Too many people feel that they're not needed. Other people, your father for instance, feel that they're supermen because they're rich. It's going to take good teachers to inform today's kids that everyone is important, that there are no supermen."

"If you feel so strongly about this, why aren't you in the teaching field?" Jess tried to squelch the irritation from her voice. Was Johnny trying to goad her by criticizing her father?

"I am preparing to do just that. I plan to follow the example set by my ancestors."

"The whatcha-ma-call-its?" Jess asked.

"The *kahunas*. Priests. Teachers. Advisors to kings. They were great, but I must be greater. I must be strong enough to make people see beyond the sham of our present-day life. I must make them understand that they must simplify."

"You sound like Thoreau," Jess said. "Don't tell me the whole Pacific Ocean is your special pond?"

"Could be." Johnny laughed, then he became serious again. "Kids today don't realize that success is no god. People who have failed but who have done their best are right on."

"Right on what?" Jess asked, chewing a crust of bread. "Right on oblivion?"

"The men in big business today are vocational snobs. I can't think of a half-dozen who don't look down on the way other men make their living."

"Maybe you're overly sensitive," Jess suggested, thinking of Johnny's beach boy status.

"The world's built on the division of labor. Each job done with honesty and diligence contributes to the sum total of human welfare."

Johnny sounded as if he were quoting from a book, and Jess squirmed. "I'm sure you have a good point, Johnny. I won't argue with you." She grinned up at him. "The world would be a far worse place without beach boys to take girls surfing and to feed them hard rolls and cheese on a white sand beach."

"Do me a favor, Jess. Apply for a teaching job here on Oahu. I'll take you for an interview on your lunch hour. What do you say?"

"I admire your sincerity, Johnny. But let me think it over." Suddenly Jess wished she were at home, at the Wong house. She had endured a most disturbing day, and now she needed solitude. Where did her allegiance lie? She hated being put in the position of spying, yet she owed a debt to her father. Of course she wasn't sure that Johnny Kuhio was the one leaking information to Pine Pack's competitors. Just because he openly talked against her father was no reason to suspect him of giving away trade secrets.

Jess felt guilty because she was so attracted to Johnny although she knew of his negative attitude toward her father. And she felt even more guilty when she realized that she disliked Reeta McQuigg and secretly hoped that she was the one who would lose her job over the public relations leaks.

Perhaps teaching would be her answer, her escape from this unfortunate situation. If a teaching position presented itself, her father would want her to take it. His letter had said that. He had invited her to work at Pine Pack until the time that she found a place in her chosen profession.

"How about it, Jess? Will you let me take you classroom hunting? I can borrow a jeep from the hotel."

Jess sighed. "All right, Johnny. I'll go. But you've got to promise to keep it a secret. I want no one at Pine Pack, and that includes my dad, to know I've looked elsewhere for a job."

"I get the message." Johnny grinned. "You might say that it would be bad public relations."

Jess sat on the beach with Johnny until the stars pricked the night and the moon hung like a medallion in the sky. Later, they walked home. It was over two miles to the Wong mansion, but Jess enjoyed every step of the way. When they reached her front door Johnny kissed her good night, and she responded to the warmth of his lips.

Slipping quietly to her room, Jess lay down on her bed to think. Was she falling in love? But how silly! She had only known Johnny Kuhio since yesterday. Love couldn't happen that rapidly. And she really didn't want to fall in love with a beach boy scholar, a radical who talked sense one minute and nonsense the next.

Why had she agreed to go school hunting with him? Why? She wanted to teach, but maybe the desire to escape Reeta McQuigg's company, to escape the problems waiting at Pine Pack, influenced her thinking. One thing for sure, she had to think for herself. She couldn't let her father or Johnny Kuhio or Reeta McQuigg be responsible for her decisions. She vowed to be her own woman.

Chapter Six

The next two weeks flew by as swiftly as gulls on the trade winds. Although Jess matched herself to the work pace in the public relations office, she felt as if she were being swept along by a high tide of activity.

The more Jess saw of Johnny Kuhio, the more she enjoyed his company. And each day Alex impressed her with his charm and his efficiency. The two times he had asked her for dates she had turned him down. After all, Malia had seen him first. But sometimes circumstances made it necessary for her to go out with him to cover PR assignments for evening events. She and Alex had attended the Pine Pack Surfer's annual banquet, and they had covered a speech presented by Pine Pack's personnel manager to the Rotary Club. Public relations work stimulated Jess; she was never bored.

Jess tried to forget about the information leaks from the PR office, but one morning her father mentioned them as he, Jess, and Malia lingered over breakfast coffee.

"I hate to rush you, Jess, but have you any

idea who may be giving away our PR ideas?"

"None." Jess stirred her coffee. "Everyone seems devoted to his job."

"What about Johnny Kuhio?" her father asked. "He's my prime suspect. I know you've been dating him."

"That's an unfair question, Dad." Malia brushed a long strand of hair over the shoulder of her orange and chartreuse muumuu. "You can't expect Jess to tattle on her friends. Half the girls I know would like to be dating Johnny Kuhio."

"That beach bum!" Mr. Wong scowled. "Jess! I thought maybe you were going with him to see what you could find out. Not true?"

"Not true," Jess agreed. "I like Johnny very much. His ideas are unique and far out. Sometimes we argue a lot, but you said you were interested in creative people — in people who think differently."

"I certainly don't consider Kuhio a creative thinker." Mr. Wong jumped up from the table and began pacing. "His ideas differ from mine, that's for sure. But he conforms to his own group. As long as his beach bum friends think as he does, he's full of assurance. But he wouldn't dare express a thought that differed from theirs. You can believe that!"

"If you'd rather I didn't see him . . ." Jess let her voice fade away.

"Oh, no. No." Mr. Wong sat down again. "I won't dictate your private life any more than I'd dictate Malia's. I certainly don't expect her to stop seeing Alex. And he could be the one. No, as long as Johnny does a good job on the paper, I won't complain."

"He does a superior job," Malia said. "You've told me so yourself. You said that the paper has never been better."

"Okay. So he does a superior job. So I'm stuck with him for a year. But I don't have to like him. Jess, what about Reeta and Alex? Have you noticed anything unusual about their actions? Or have you overheard any suspicious talk?"

"None, Dad. I really don't think Reeta's the career girl type. I get the impression that she's just putting in time until the right man comes along. But that can hardly be considered subversive thinking."

"Right," Mr. Wong agreed. "And Alex?"

"In my opinion Alex is really dedicated to you, to you and to the company."

"I'm glad to hear that," Mr. Wong said. "That's the impression that I have of him. And if everything goes well, he's in line for a big promotion soon."

"He's already head of the PR depart-

84

ment," Malia said. "What promotion do you have in mind? He hasn't told me about it, and I was out with him just last night."

"He doesn't know about it yet. It's top secret, you understand, but I have him in mind for head of the advertising department. Advertising goes right along with public relations."

"Dad! That's wonderful!" Malia exclaimed.

"Then who'll head the PR office?" Jess asked. "Reeta?"

"Are you interested in the position?"

"Dad! You're joking! I hardly know my way around the office."

"Yes, I'm joking. But only for the time being. You'll learn, Jess. You're catching on fast. If I do give Alex the promotion, I'll probably take over the PR duties myself. At least for a while."

"That's too much of a load, Dad," Malia protested.

"You seem to forget that I started Pine Pack single-handed. I used to do all the work on the management end of the stick. And PR was always my favorite field." Mr. Wong glanced at his watch and jumped up again. "Ready, Jess? We'd better get going."

Jess took a moment to dash to her room, to apply fresh lipstick, to run a comb through her hair, and a few moments later she was the first one to step into the PR office. How quiet it was.

Jess glanced at the four desks in the room and smiled. Each one expressed the personality of its owner. Johnny's desktop was a dusty jumble of papers, books, glossies. Alex's desk reflected his organizational ability. An in basket and an out basket sat on one end of the desk, and a pencil caddy and a letter file on the other end gave the work space a balanced look. Reeta's desk was polished to a high gloss, but it was bare except for a low milk-glass bowl containing a single white carnation.

Jess sat down at her own desk only moments before Johnny entered the office. By the time she had checked her appointment calendar he was bringing her the galleys for the next issue of his paper.

"Seems as if I just finished proofing those galleys." Jess glanced over the slick sheets.

"It's like washing dishes," Johnny said with a grin. "As soon as you get one batch cleaned up, there's another batch waiting for you."

"I'll get busy on them right away." Jess took her green ballpoint from her desk drawer, hoping Johnny would go on about his work. But he remained by her side.

"Ready for your school interview this noon?"

Jess nodded. She had written to the school superintendent at Johnny's urging, and his reply had been prompt.

"The interview won't come to anything, Johnny. Superintendent Higgins said there were no openings."

"But he also said that he'd put your name on a waiting list." Urgency penetrated the liquid smoothness of Johnny's voice. "You have to start somewhere." Pulling an orchid blossom from behind his ear, he tucked it into Jess's hair. "See you at noon."

Jess spent an hour proofing the galleys. The work went more quickly now that she was becoming familiar with the proper names of the Pine Pack personnel. She had just placed the finished sheets in her out basket when Reeta approached.

"Time for some legwork, Jess." Reeta ran her hand over her platinum hair, which she had piled in a bun high on her head. "Kelli Puno out in the cannery is the proud father of a baby boy. His first. I want you to get the basic facts so I can put the story on our weekly radio program."

"Okay." Jess grabbed a notebook and stood. "What do I ask him?"

"Just the basics. You know. Who? What?

87

When? Where? What are you waiting for?"

"Nothing," Jess said. "Nothing at all." She pulled a ballpoint from her desk drawer, tested the point on her notebook, then headed for the door. This was her first solo assignment out of the office, and her stomach suddenly felt as if she had swallowed a tangled skein of yarn.

"Buck up," Alex said as she passed his desk. "Kelli hasn't bitten anyone in all the years I've worked here."

"But he may feel hungry today." Jess grinned.

"Just be friendly and relaxed, and he'll probably talk you to death."

Jess smiled her thanks to Alex and left the office. The silence of the outer corridor and the steep stairway was like a protective shield, but when she opened the heavy door that separated the offices from the cannery, noise pounded at her from all sides. Kelli Puno stood in his usual place manning the spraying equipment, and Jess approached him with a lilting step and a smile.

"Mr. Puno!" Jess shouted above the splashing of the water and the thump of pineapples hitting a conveyor belt. "The PR office needs some information about your new baby."

"What's that?" Mr. Puno shouted and

cupped his hand around his right ear.

"Your new baby!" Jess shouted again. "When was it born? Where? How much did it weigh?"

Mr. Puno started to shout again, then he shook his head and motioned for her to give him the notebook and pen. Jess obliged. When Mr. Puno finished writing he grinned at Jess, and again his plump cheeks almost hid his eyes. Mr. Pineapple, Jess nicknamed him in her mind as she stood on tip-toe to read what he had written.

Born 4:00 A.M. today. Mercy Hospital. Weight — six pounds ten ounces.

"What's his name?" Jess shouted.

"David." Mr. Puno wrote the name down. "A good name for a boy."

"Thank you very much." Jess shouted again just as some machinery ceased to operate. Her voice carried through the vast expanse of the cannery. With a burning face she lowered her voice. "We'll have an announcement on the radio program. Be sure to listen."

Mr. Puno beamed his pleasure, and Jess hurried back to the PR office and dropped her information onto Reeta's desk. No one was in the office, but through the window she saw Alex and Reeta having coffee on the employees' lanai. At first she was tempted to join them, but then she saw a new paper on her desk with a note clipped to the top.

"Jess. This the story on the Kapalana twins' new handmade catamaran. Johnny had to go out to check another story, and he wants you to verify this one. Have each twin read and initial it."

The second time she entered the cannery Jess was more at ease. Mr. Pineapple waved to her and she waved back. Conscious of many eyes following her, Jess hurried to the area where the Kapalana twins inspected cored fruit. A whistle blew to announce coffee break, and Jess grinned at the brothers. "May I share a few moments of your time?"

"It's our pleasure, miss." Just one of the twins spoke, but they both smiled, revealing crescents of white teeth.

"Johnny Kuhio would like your okay on this story for the company paper. If you have additions or corrections, please make note of them on the reverse side of the sheet. Your catamaran sounds fabulous."

"She's a good one all right," Fred Kapalana replied. "We think she'll win."

"Win what?" Jess asked.

"The catamaran races next week," Ned Kapalana answered. "We represent Pine Pack."

Jess felt her face flush. She should have read Johnny's story before she brought it for the twins to sign. "I'd like to see the races," she said. "They sound exciting."

Both twins initialed the story, and Jess hurried back to her office, dropping the catamaran copy onto Johnny's desk as she passed it.

Alex and Reeta were back in their places, and Reeta picked up another sheaf of papers and headed toward Jess. "This copy has to be proofed some time today. It's tricky — lots of numbers and dates. Better get right on it."

"But not until you've had your coffee break." Alex joined the girls. "We're really not slave drivers around here. Take a few minutes off, Jess."

"Thanks, but it's almost noon right now. I'll skip my break for this morning."

"Then take fifteen extra at noon," Alex insisted. "You deserve it."

"Thanks, Alex. I'll see how it goes."

Jess was deep into the proofing when Johnny stopped at her desk. "You one wahine work too hard. Bimeby you see how silly. Time for da kine lunch break. Wahine come wid me."

"Practicing for your beach boy chores?" Jess laughed and laid the copy on her desk.

"Johnny Kuhio try to give de tourist ladies what dey expect. Pidgin is it."

"Your hotel would probably lose business if the girls found out you already have three college degrees and are working on a fourth." Jess laughed.

"Come on. Let's get out of here. I've borrowed a hotel jeep for exactly one hour."

"Give me time to fix my face." Jess took her purse from her desk drawer and hurried to the ladies' room. How she wished she had never promised Johnny to follow through on this interview. She was really quite happy working at Pine Pack. She was learning the routine from the ground up, and the more she learned the better she liked it.

Once out in the sunshine Jess saw Johnny sitting behind the wheel of a jeep. The top was made of pink and white striped canvas, and on each side of the vehicle signs proclaimed the superiority of the Surfside Hotel.

"What will Superintendent Higgins think of an applicant who arrives in a jeep?" Jess grinned.

"He'll think you need the job so you can buy a decent car," Johnny replied. "Do you have your transcript of grades? Your social security number?"

Jess patted her purse. "Everything's right here."

They drove along the beach highway, and Jess thought she would never tire of watching the waves scallop the sand, of watching the palms dip toward the water. But Johnny soon turned the jeep inland, and for a few miles the overgrown tropical thicket cut off the trade winds. The jeep grew hot, and the day became humid.

"There's the school." Johnny nodded to their right. "I'll park right by the door. You run in and turn on the charm."

"Superintendents seem to be more interested in grades than in charm." Jess grinned as she climbed from the jeep. Hurrying into the schoolhouse she found that the superintendent's office was right across from the entrance. As she stepped through the doorway, a tall, balding man rose to greet her.

"You must be Miss Wong. I'm Mr. Higgins. Please have a chair. I'm really afraid that you've come all this distance for no real purpose."

"Perhaps so," Jess replied. "I know that your school year is well under way, but I would like to be considered should a vacancy arise."

"Of course." Mr. Higgins pulled at his right earlobe as if he were uneasy in her presence. "May I see your transcript?"

Jess pulled the Xerox copy of her grades from her purse and handed it to him. Then she studied him as he studied her grades. After a few moments the schoolbell rang, bringing them both to attention.

"You have excellent grades, Miss Wong. I'll certainly keep you in mind if we have any vacancies. Could you give me three names of reference?"

Jess hesitated. "I am a newcomer to the islands. Any names I could give would be of people in New York."

"I thought you might be related to the Wong who runs Pine Pack," Mr. Higgins said.

"Rick Wong is my father," Jess replied. "But please! I want to keep this interview confidential. I work at Pine Pack, and my father might be hurt if he thought I was actively seeking another job."

"I understand," Mr. Higgins said. "Our meeting will be our secret."

Jess wrote down the names and addresses of three people in New York who would vouch for her, then, after thanking Mr. Higgins, she hurried from his office and ran back to Johnny in the jeep.

"Thank goodness that's over! Somehow I feel like a real heel, Johnny. Dad wants me to teach if I want to, but I feel that I've done this behind his back."

"You did the right thing," Johnny insisted. "The world needs dedicated teachers. Education is the answer to all problems."

On the return ride to Pine Pack, Johnny pulled the jeep into a secluded area far back from the beach. "I want to show you something here, Jess. Get out a minute."

Jess jumped from the jeep and frowned at her watch. She hated to be late getting back to work, even though Alex had allowed her an extra fifteen minutes.

"Look right here." Johnny pointed to a level square of ground with indentations at its four corners. "A *heiau* once stood here — a temple where my great-grandfather worshipped."

"How can you be sure?" Jess asked.

"When I was a child, my great-grandfather brought me here. He could remember the days of the kahunas. There used to be a tower with three platforms here. The bottom platform represented earth. People placed their offerings to the gods on it. The second platform was higher up and it represented heaven. My kahuna ancestors used the second platform for regular worship. The third platform was reserved for the High Kahuna or for the king himself. My ancestors induced self-hypnosis so that the voices of the gods would flow through them and advise their people of wise actions."

Johnny's smooth voice almost hypnotized Jess. In her mind she saw the ancient temple, the wise priests.

"I am a descendant of the great kahunas," Johnny said. "One day the people of Hawaii will hear their voices through me. I will lead the dispossessed back to a kind of nonpower, back to the old ways of happiness and freedom."

"You're a dreamer," Jess said. "You can't really believe what you're saying."

"I believe. You're the one who doubts." Johnny scowled. "Come on. Let's get you back to the office and me back to the hotel where Hawaiian beach boys belong."

Chapter Seven

One morning after Jess had been with Pine Pack for over three months, her father strode into the PR office with a manila folder in his hand and a determined look in his eye. Reeta, Johnny, and Alex snapped to attention as if someone had blown a bugle.

"What is it, sir?" Alex stepped forward. "Have we overlooked something?"

"Relax." Mr. Wong smiled. "All of you. Get out paper and pencil and come with me to the lanai. This meeting may take a while and we may as well be comfortable. Bring coffee, if you want it."

While the others were getting notebooks and pencils, Jess wanted to run to her father and ask him what was up. He had mentioned nothing unusual at the breakfast table that morning. Had he discovered who was divulging Pine Pack business ideas?

Johnny stopped at Jess's desk. "Hurry up. When the old man speaks, he expects action. Chop. Chop. The paper. Chop. Chop. To the lanai."

"You know he isn't as bad as all that."

Jess grinned up at Johnny as they left the office.

Once they were seated on the flagged terrace, Mr. Wong got to the point of his impromptu meeting. "I want a new and fresh PR approach, and I want it aimed at our four major publics."

"Publics?" Jess blurted the word — then she wished she could drag it back as Reeta glared at her and Alex smiled like a parent enjoying the innocence of a young child.

"Publics." Her father repeated the word. "Plural. A public is a particular group of people, and our society is composed of many publics. We are interested in four major groups: the community, the consumers, the planters, and the cannery workers."

Jess jotted the words down, but she was the only one taking notes. The others sat at attention, listening.

"Pine Pack needs to show goodwill toward the community," Mr. Wong said. "We need to let the Honolulu citizens know that we appreciate being able to make a living here. A company that works at fostering good community relations shows that it cares about local people, and it's a fact that when a company prospers, so does the community nearest it."

"And when a community prospers, so does a company," Alex said. "It works both ways."

"Right." Mr. Wong rose and paced the lanai, sloshing coffee from his cup as he went. "The second public we must reach is the consumer. Work in this area may be more difficult, as most of our consumers are over two thousand miles away on the mainland. We must ask ourselves what the consumer wants, then we must supply sufficiently to meet his demands. We need ideas that will promote sales and that at the same time will show appreciation.

"Closer at hand we need to aim a campaign at our planters and at our cannery workers. We should let them know they are necessary and that management cares about them. So far we've tried to express our interest through *Pine Pack News*, through management letters to all personnel, and through company movies. But now I want something new and different."

Mr. Wong stopped speaking and only the call of a dove broke the silence on the lanai. At last Alex said, "We haven't held an open house for a long time. Or we might think about organizing some new inter-company sport activities."

"Don't tell me your ideas yet," Mr. Wong

said. "But pigeonhole them in your minds. I want each of you to think about Pine Pack and about Pine Pack's publics for twenty-four hours. At this same time tomorrow morning we'll meet here again for a general discussion group. I'll expect to hear from each of you. We'll toss your ideas around and work from there. In the meantime remember that everyone wants to be a part of the team. Everyone wants to be needed and necessary. That's all for this morning. You may go back to your desks."

Mr. Wong hurried away before anyone could ask questions, and Johnny stood by Jess until she gathered her things and stood.

"Well, Big Boss has spoken. Did he set your brain to spinning?"

"I'm afraid not." Jess laughed. "I wish there were a cute little idea bar at the nearest department store where I could buy a supply of fresh thoughts."

"I'm going to suggest that he put pineapple juice in the coffee machines," Johnny said. "For free, of course."

Jess was glad when they returned to office routine and Johnny settled down to work on his paper. She arranged some pamphlets in front of herself and pretended to be reading them, but her mind strayed. Her dad's push for new ideas was the beginning of the end for someone. But for whom? After three months in the office Jess still had no idea of who was the guilty person. Perhaps her dad was mistaken. Maybe the past information leaks had been accidental. The mail boy could have overheard something on his rounds, and in order to make himself seem important and in the know, he could have mentioned what he heard in the wrong places.

Or an information leak could have come directly from the Wong home. Ora and Malia both had access to her dad's office. One of them could have accidentally talked about secret matters. Jess sighed. She was grasping at slim possibilities.

"Jess." Reeta walked toward her, heels tapping on the bare floor. "I want you to write a release about the new labels for Pine Pack's number two cans. The information's all here in this folder. The story will go to the local paper. It'll help prepare the public for the new look the labels will create. See what you can do with it."

"I'll try." Jess smiled at Reeta, then opened the folder and began studying the contents. As soon as she felt that she was familiar with the facts, she began writing, composing directly on the typewriter. She spent an hour on the rough draft before she revised it with ballpoint, read it half-aloud to herself, then retyped it and repeated the whole process a second time.

While she worked she imagined she could feel Reeta's eyes boring into her back, but Reeta didn't hurry her. Jess knew she worked slowly. But writing a release was a new endeavor, and she wanted to do a good job. At last she read the copy once again, then she placed it on Reeta's desk.

"Wait," Reeta called as Jess started to leave. "I'll proofread this immediately and you can take it to Mr. Wong for final approval." Reeta's eyes darted over the copy. She made a few penciled corrections then looked up at Jess and smiled. "This is a good effort. I think it'll do. Take it in to Mr. Wong, please."

Reeta usually gave praise like a miser gave ten-dollar bills, and Jess felt a glow of pride as she walked to her dad's office. Her dad was out, so Jess placed the copy on the middle of his desk blotter where he'd be sure to see it. When she returned to her own desk, she began working once more on the company brochure that had occupied her spare moments for the past three months. She almost had a tentative outline ready for Alex's approval. She glanced at her watch. There was a chance that she would finish it that day.

Jess was so deep in concentration that she jumped when her father entered the office and waved her news story under Reeta's nose.

"This will never do, Miss McQuigg. Never. I've seldom read such a poorly constructed story. Only a complete rewrite will save it."

"Perhaps you'll want to talk to Jess." Reeta purred words. "She did this assignment. I'm sure she did her best."

"Didn't you recheck it before she brought it to me?"

"She must have slipped it to you before I had a chance to go over it," Reeta said.

A knot of anger tightened in Jess's stomach as she heard Reeta's lie. Her father's displeasure mortified her.

"Come into my office, Jess," her father said. "We'll discuss this in there."

Feeling like a disobedient child who had been called to the principal's office, Jess obeyed. She glared at Reeta as she passed her desk, but Reeta's face was an immobile mask.

"Now don't panic, Jess," her father said as they sat down in his office. "This is your first news release."

Jess nodded. "I'm sorry it doesn't suit

you. I won't mind doing it over once I know what to do to improve it."

"There are good things about the article," Mr. Wong said. "It presents news. That's the first essential. A news release must always be news or create news. And the timing is on target. A release about a new or improved product must coincide with its availability locally. Your article meets that requirement. The new labels will appear in Honolulu stores day after tomorrow."

Jess's shoulders slumped. "Reeta saw to those things. I only did the writing, and that's what's bad."

"It's not bad, Jess, but it is poorly organized. We never know how much space the paper will allot us for any release. So it's essential to write sparingly, to cover all the facts — the who, what, when, where, why — in the first paragraph. You've included all those facts in this release, but they're spread throughout several paragraphs. If the news editor cuts the copy, something vital will go."

"I'll reorganize it," Jess said.

"It won't be difficult," her father said. "After you state the five essentials in the first paragraph, then use as many names as you can. This adds human interest to the release, and it pleases the people whose names appear. Take it back and run it through your typewriter one more time, then show it to me before you leave."

Jess took the copy and returned to her desk. She saw Reeta through a red miasma of anger. Reeta had deliberately done this to her, deliberately let her make a fool of herself before her father. And then she had lied about it. Jess didn't realize how hard she was banging the typewriter keys until Alex stopped at her desk.

"Got a personal grudge against the machine?" he asked.

Jess forced a smile. "Not really. I'm just in a hurry to get this copy on Dad's desk before quitting time. By the way, I have the outline for a new employees' brochure ready for your inspection. Want to see it today?"

"Sure thing." Alex took the sheets Jess had clipped together and returned to his own desk to examine them.

As soon as Jess finished the rewrite of the news release, she bypassed Reeta and carried it directly to her father.

"Wait, Jess." Mr. Wong paced as he read. "It'll only take me a moment to go over this."

Jess didn't realize she was holding her breath until her dad spoke again.

"Good girl. This is professionally done.

Your first story would have been nothing but a throwaway when it reached the news editor's desk. But this one will be published. There's no doubt about it."

"Thanks, Dad. I'd like to write some more releases now that I'm getting the hang of it."

"I'll see that Reeta gives you some assignments. Are you ready to leave for the day?"

"Not quite." Jess glanced at her watch. "I want to check with Alex on the employees' brochure. The outline's on his desk right now."

Jess left her dad's office, and the moment she stepped back into the PR room, Alex motioned to her.

"This outline covers the material, Jess. But I have some changes to suggest in the format. If you'll have dinner with me tonight, I'll discuss them with you. How about it? I know it can wait until tomorrow, but tomorrow will be devoted almost entirely to the special meeting — the idea exchange. I'd like to take you to dinner."

Jess wished she had the willpower to refuse. She knew Malia liked Alex, although they both dated others. But after all, this was business, wasn't it? Lots of co-workers had business lunches and dinners together.

"All right, Alex. I'd enjoy having dinner

with you. I'll stick the outline in my purse."

"Fine. Pick you up around seven. Okay?"

Jess nodded and for a moment she felt bubbly and excited, but on the ride home with her father, her spirits drooped. She could only think of Malia. She wouldn't go out with Alex behind Malia's back. She wouldn't be sneaky. As soon as she stepped into the house she headed for Malia's room and tapped gently on the door.

"Come in," Malia called. "Have a good day?"

Jess stepped through the doorway and picked her way through a maze of shoes, books, and jewelry that had fallen in Malia's wake.

"A busy day." Jess sighed. "I've something to tell you."

"It can't be as bad as all that. You look as if you'd lost your last dollar."

"Alex asked me out to dinner tonight and I accepted. It's supposed to be business, but. . . . I just don't know how you feel about him, Malia. I know you date lots of other boys, but if you'd rather I didn't go out with him . . ."

For a moment Malia stood statue still, but when she spoke her voice shook. "You've a perfect right to have dinner with anyone you choose, Jess. You certainly don't have to ask my permission. But I'm busy right now and I'd appreciate it if you'd leave me alone."

Jess stepped from Malia's room as stunned as if her sister had hit her. Why had she even mentioned her dinner with Alex? Why hadn't she just gone with him and kept the evening on a strictly business level? Why? Because she liked Alex, that's why. And because she hadn't known how Malia felt about him. But now she knew.

Jess stepped to the telephone in its niche in the corridor, fumbled in the directory, then dialed Alex's home number.

"Is Alex there, please?" she asked the strange voice that answered her ring. "Oh, when do you expect him? Thank you. I'll call again."

Jess replaced the receiver, but before she could disappear into her room, Malia called to her.

"I'm sorry I lost my temper, Jess."

"I'm the one who should apologize," Jess said. "I just tried to call Alex to break our date."

"Don't do it," Malia said. "Don't do it."

"But I don't want to start any trouble be-tween you and Alex. Or between you and me. Alex isn't that important to me."

"I'll level with you, Jess. Of all the boys I date, Alex is my favorite. But he goes out with lots of other girls, and I try not to resent them. I want you to go out with him if you want to. What fun would it be for me to date him thinking that perhaps he prefers your company but that you bowed out of the picture to pave the way for me? That's not how I want to play the game. You go out with him. If it's business, okay. If it's pleasure, okay."

"Malia, you're quite a girl." Jess grinned at her sister. "Right now I'm really fond of Johnny Kuhio, and I don't know if I could have such a generous attitude to the other girls who date him."

"Let's think no more of it," Malia said. "I'm going out tonight with Penni Larando. He plays oboe in the symphony, and we have lots in common."

Malia returned to her room, and Jess tried to rest for a few moments before it was time to dress for dinner. But the more she thought about Alex, the more excited she became. He wasn't as handsome as Johnny, but he always left her feeling that he had unplumbed depths to his personality. She was eager to know him better.

Chapter Eight

Jess brushed her hair and gazed into her open closet trying to decide what to wear. If only Alex had said where they would go for dinner! She tossed her hairbrush onto the bed and pulled out an ankle-length Chinese dress with the skirt slit to the knee. This will do, she thought, glad that Malia had gone shopping with her, had helped her choose a basic wardrobe suitable for the islands.

When the doorbell rang, Jess dashed to the entryway before Ora could answer the summons and invite Alex inside. She smiled and patted the huge straw bag that matched her sandals. "I have the brochure outline right here in my purse."

"We'll get to that later." Alex grinned at her. "Pleasure before business is the order of the evening. Where would you like to eat?"

"You choose," Jess said. "I've been to so few restaurants that any one you pick will be a treat."

Alex opened the car door and helped Jess inside. "In that case I choose The Top of Waikiki." Alex walked around the car and slid under the wheel. "It's a revolving restaurant on the top of the Parker Building."

"Sounds great," Jess said. "I've never been in a revolving restaurant." She relaxed on the short ride to the shopping center where Alex parked the car. They walked half a block to the Parker Building and took an elevator to the restaurant. Alex smiled at the headwaiter.

"Mr. Yanagisako! Good evening." The headwaiter straightened his brightly flowered cummerbund as he approached them. "A table for two?"

"Please, Renni," Alex said.

The headwaiter checked the empty tables in the restaurant, then he checked his reservation sheet. "If only you had called ahead . . ."

"I know I should have," Alex replied. "But we made a spur-of-the-moment decision."

"Can you wait fifteen minutes?" the headwaiter asked.

Alex grinned. "Sure. We're here for the evening."

"Fine," the headwaiter said. "If you'd like to take seats in the lounge, we'll have a table for you soon."

"Sorry, Jess," Alex said as they settled down to wait. "Are you starving?"

"There's so much to see up here, that I forgot I was hungry." Jess smiled and watched two girls dressed in the soft-folded saris of India cross the lounge. Three other women in long, full-skirted muumuus waited near the elevator. All around them the smell of fresh gardenias and plumeria perfumed the air.

It seemed to Jess that they had only begun to wait when the headwaiter summoned them to a table. After they sat down, Jess gazed out at the Pacific Ocean and then back at Alex.

"How did you manage to get us a table by the window?"

"I wouldn't have any other kind," Alex said. "In the hour or so that we'll sit here, this spot will offer a complete 360-degree view from the mountains to the sea."

"I can't see Diamond Head," Jess said.

"Not at the moment. You're looking at Barber's Point. Diamond Head will appear later. This table will make a full circle of the Ala Moana Tower."

"I've never been anywhere as wonderful as this," Jess said. "But seeing such a vast amount of sky and sea makes me feel like a very small speck in the universe."

"You're a very large item in my universe." Alex smiled. Then he paused as the head-waiter approached.

"Would you care for drinks from our bar?"

"Will you join me in a glass of wine, Jess?" Jess nodded.

"My special vintage, Renni." Alex looked up at the headwaiter. "And please let us scan the menu while you're gone."

Renni placed menus before them and left them alone.

"I wanted you to have plenty of time to study the cuisine," Alex explained. "Many of these choices may be unfamiliar to you."

Alex's sophistication impressed Jess. Clearly he had been here many times before. But with whom? Malia? Maybe Reeta?

"Is there any special dinner that you recommend?" Jess asked as she studied the menu.

Alex shook his head. "If you like exotic dining, you're in the right place. Or if you prefer familiar food, they have that too. The Mandarin and Cantonese cooking is excellent here, but I prefer the piquant flavors of Japanese food. Take your choice."

Jess studied the menu again. "I think I'll try Filipino arroz de Valenciana. It says in parentheses that it's chicken rice. And I'll try Portuguese sweetbread. Does that sound okay?"

"Very okay." Alex scanned the menu a while longer, and when Renni arrived with their wine, he ordered the chicken for Jess and a sukiyaki dinner for himself.

By the time their meals arrived it was dark, and Jess watched flickering torches cast wavering shadows far below them on some hotel lanai. Alex pointed out certain lights and landmarks to her as they ate, and Jess felt as if she had been whisked into another world. She could easily understand why Alex was Malia's favorite escort.

Idly Jess wondered if Johnny had ever eaten in this spot. She guessed that he hadn't. He would consider it enemy territory. How strange that she could understand Johnny's point of view at the very moment she was basking in Alex's attention. Yet somehow she remembered the flavor of hard rolls and cheese with an occasional grit of sand tossed in for good measure.

"Have you always lived in Honolulu?" Jess asked as they sipped their wine.

"My grandparents came here from Japan, but I've always lived here."

"How did your grandparents happen to move here?" Jess asked. "It's very far from Japan."

"Grandfather came to work the sugar fields. The Japanese were welcome enough when their only interest lay in the cane fields. But it was a different story after the attack on Pearl Harbor. Have you seen the monument to the *Arizona*?"

"Dad took me there when I first arrived," Jess said. "But surely people didn't blame your family for the Pearl Harbor attack."

"Not my family personally. They blamed all Japanese. But my father and his two brothers went to war against Japan. Of the three men my father was the only one who returned. Mother still has pictures of the victory parade down Kapiolani Boulevard. Dad was there with his medals and ribbons. I suppose my uncles would have been proud of him. He was now accepted where they had not been. It was a big price to pay."

"I didn't mean to bring up a painful subject," Jess said.

"You're forgiven." Alex smiled as Renni served their meal.

Again Jess thought that food had never tasted so good. She hated to see the meal end, hated to get down to the business part of the evening. But once Alex finished his dessert, he was ready to work.

"May I see your brochure outline once more, Jess?"

Jess pulled the papers from her purse. "Should we sit here, or should we free the table for someone else?"

"The dinner rush is over. We're welcome to linger over coffee for as long as we care to." Quickly Alex thumbed through the sheets Jess handed him, then he began to read more slowly.

"For the most part this outline is very good, Jess. A bit of rearranging will bring it in excellent order."

"What sort of rearranging do you have in mind?"

"You've put the history of Pine Pack at the beginning. I think it would work better at the end. New employees are interested in themselves. They want to know what their duties will be. They want to know the rules and regulations of their department. After that they may be interested in company history. You haven't started the actual writing yet, have you?"

"Not yet. Any changes will be easy to make at this point."

"Good. Another idea — I want you to check with the head of each of our departments. Let the supervisor read your copy. Ask his opinion. Ask for additions and suggestions. Not only will you get some new thoughts, but you'll have helped cement good relations between management and labor."

Jess admired Alex for his ideas and for his straight thinking. Good public relations just amounted to using common sense. Or perhaps it was uncommon sense. She didn't seem to find it common yet.

Suddenly Alex nudged her and nodded toward the doorway.

"Reeta," Jess said. "Who's she with?"

"Bruce Brietag. Honolulu's number one playboy."

"Brietag? Isn't that the name of the family who owns Commercial Can?" Was this a coincidence, Jess wondered.

"It's the same family," Alex replied. "But Bruce has nothing to do with the pineapple business. He manufactures perfume. Or rather he hires men to manage his perfume business for him. Oh, oh. They're coming our way."

Inwardly Jess cringed as Reeta and her escort headed toward them. As usual Reeta wore white. This time her costume was an ankle-length pantdress with metallic threads that shimmered in the light whenever she moved. Her silvery hair cascaded down her back in a loose fall, and a heavy touch of eye makeup was the only color that accented her face.

"I love it when we meet someone here that we know," Reeta purred. "May we join you?" She batted her long lashes at Alex, and they were so blatantly false that they reminded Jess of black centipede legs. She watched Reeta's escort for his reaction to her meeting with Alex, but Bruce Brietag seemed not to notice that his date was throwing herself at another man.

"We're just leaving, Reeta," Alex said. "But you may have our table. The view is the greatest." Alex stood and Jess followed his lead, amazed that anyone could say no in such a charming manner.

"How was that for some fast thinking?" Alex asked when they were safely in the elevator.

"You dislike Reeta?" Jess asked.

"I didn't say that. I just didn't plan to turn our evening into a cozy foursome. Hope you don't mind."

"I see quite enough of Reeta at the office." Jess sighed. "Sometimes she makes me want to resign, to make myself find a teaching job somewhere — anywhere."

"Don't you enjoy public relations work?" Alex maneuvered the car from its parking slot into the beachside traffic and headed toward Waikiki.

"I suppose it's too soon to decide for

sure," Jess said. "But I'm afraid I'm not creative enough to make the grade. In less than twelve hours I'm supposed to have some ideas for all those publics Dad spoke of this morning. So far my mind's a blank."

"Have you really thought about the situation? Have you put everything else from your mind and concentrated on one of our publics?"

"No, not really. I've been too busy with the work at the office, then thinking about this evening. Maybe that's my trouble. I really haven't taken time to concentrate on new ideas."

"I'm sure you're right. And I hope you won't be insulted if I take you straight home. I've had a great evening and I hope you have too. But I don't have any ideas for tomorrow's meeting either. But I will have by morning."

"How can you be so sure?"

"Because as soon as I take you home I intend to go home myself and start concentrating. Whenever I'm faced with a problem or a decision, I spend about an hour in deep thought on the subject just before I go to bed. Then I let my subconscious take over for the next eight hours or so. Usually by morning I find that something in my brain has clicked. I usually come up with the solution I've been needing."

"I'll give your system a try," Jess said. "I've certainly nothing to lose."

Alex parked the car in front of the Wong residence and walked to the door with Jess. He made no attempt to kiss her goodnight, and Jess thanked him for the pleasant evening and hurried on inside.

Jess hadn't been in her room more than two minutes before Malia poked her head through the doorway. At first Jess felt guilty all over again, but she tried to squelch the feeling. If she and Malia were to be friends as well as sisters, they would have to be truthful to each other.

"How was your evening?" Malia asked. "He certainly brought you home early enough."

"Alex brought me home so I could think." Jess giggled. "It's true. I have to think up some fresh ideas for Dad. But I had a grand time. We went to the revolving restaurant at the shopping center. I had a ball, but I think Alex just had a pleasant business evening. We didn't dance at all. He just went over my outline for a brochure, then . . ."

When Jess hesitated, Malia prompted her. "Then what?"

"Then Reeta McQuigg came in with

Bruce Brietag. Doesn't that strike you as strange?"

"Not especially. Why?"

"I was thinking about the information leaks that have been bothering Dad. I wonder if he knows that Reeta dates a member of his competitor's family."

"You might mention it to him," Malia suggested. "But Reeta dates lots of fellows. With her looks she can get about anyone she wants."

"Anyone except Alex. She plays up to him all day at work, and she made a grandstand play for him tonight, but he gave her the brushoff. I don't know what to make of it. He seems friendly enough to her at the office."

"PR." Malia laughed. "But what did Alex bring you home to think about?"

"Dad's called a meeting for tomorrow. We're each to present ideas for a new PR campaign. And my mind's blank. Got any ideas for cementing relations with the community?"

Malia flopped down on Jess's bed. "As a matter of fact I have. But Dad won't listen to me. If the idea came from you it might have a chance. I think Pine Pack ought to sponsor some symphony concerts. The symphony always needs money, and it provides cultural events that appeal to citizens of Honolulu as well as to the tourists."

"Sounds as if it might work," Jess said. "But I've no idea of the costs involved. I'm sure that's a factor in any decision that's made. I'll be more than glad to present the idea at the meeting. It may be the only one I'll have."

"Thanks, Jess." Malia stood. "I've got to get to bed and let you get on with your thinking. See you tomorrow."

Jess got ready for bed and when she lay stretched between the sheets she tried to forget about Alex, about Johnny, about Reeta. She tried to concentrate on getting an idea for a PR campaign.

Maybe Pine Pack could sponsor a series of symphony concerts and let a service organization sell tickets to raise money for charity. That would build good will between Pine Pack and the service organization as well as between the cannery and the residents of Honolulu. Jess smiled. At least a part of the idea was her own.

Jess stared into the darkness for many minutes, but no more ideas came to her. She tried to picture the cannery workers, the plantation growers, the consumers on the mainland. But everything was a blur in her mind as she fell into a fitful sleep.

Chapter Nine

The following morning Jess awakened to the sound of doves calling on her lanai. She shut off the alarm on her clock before it jangled and wondered why she was thinking of Johnny. Had she been dreaming of him? When she tried to pinpoint her thoughts, the image of a small girl releasing a helium-filled balloon floated across her mind. Jess wondered idly if the girl had ever written her story and if her friends had enjoyed reading it.

As Jess came fully awake she remembered the problem confronting her today. The PR idea exchange. She had so little to offer that she couldn't blame her dad if he showed his disappointment in her. And the one idea she planned to present at the meeting really belonged to Malia.

Jess jumped as someone knocked on her door. Opening it a crack she saw Ora in the hallway carrying a tray.

"I bring breakfast to you this morning," Ora said. "Mr. Wong left early for the work. He say you to take taxi. I bring breakfast early. Much early so you won't be late for work." Ora darted into the room as Jess opened the door wider. She set her tray on Jess's desk, then smoothed the skirt of her lavender uniform. "Guava juice this morning. And Portuguese sweetbread."

"It smells and looks delicious, Ora." Jess laughed to think that before last night she had never heard of Portuguese sweetbread, and now she would have eaten it twice in Jess than a day's time. "Thank you so much for bringing the tray. Is Malia up yet?"

"Up and gone off to university for early practice. Sometimes she do this." Ora shooed the gray doves from the lanai doorway, then with bracelets tinkling she darted on about her business.

Jess sat down at her desk, welcoming the opportunity to eat alone and to think about the upcoming PR campaign. She was so deep in her thoughts that she almost forgot to call a taxi. Glancing at her watch, she dashed to the telephone. And she was lucky. The cab arrived in less than five minutes and she got to Pine Pack with time to spare. Reeta was the only one in the office.

"Good morning, Jess." Reeta dusted her desk with a white tissue then wiped her fingers on a damp sponge which she kept in her desk drawer. "I was really surprised to see you and Alex last night. Did you have a good time?"

"The best." Jess checked her schedule for the day, determined not to discuss her evening with Alex. "Where will the meeting be held this morning? Have you seen Dad yet?"

"I saw him arrive a few minutes ago. I think he intends to hold the meeting in this room. The lanai is more comfortable, but the office is more businesslike."

The mail boy arrived and for a few moments he saved Jess from having to make more conversation with Reeta. But he soon left, and Reeta continued.

"You act as if you're eager for the meeting to begin, Jess. Did you come up with a big idea for us?"

"I'm afraid not." Jess shook her head. "The only thing I'm going to suggest is that Pine Pack might sponsor some symphony concerts. A service club could sell the concert tickets and use the money for charity."

"Sounds good," Reeta said.

"What have you thought of?" Jess asked, surprised that Reeta seemed so friendly.

Reeta opened her mouth to reply, but just then the mail boy returned and sorted through the mail he had left only moments ago.

"Dropped some things in here by mistake," he said, ignoring Reeta's stare. "This stuff goes to Personnel."

Jess noticed that Reeta was as careful as she not to discuss their ideas in front of the mail boy. Was Reeta aware that he might be suspect? Jess could only guess at the answer to that one, because just then Alex and her father and his secretary entered the office intent on business.

"If you girls are ready we'll get right down to the work at hand," Mr. Wong said. He raised his eyebrows as Johnny stepped into the office, obviously late for work, but he went on speaking of business. "I hope you've come up with some good ideas. Miss Punako will take notes; everyone will have a chance to present his ideas. Alex, let's start with you. What new thoughts have you had?"

Alex pulled a slim gold notebook from his jacket pocket and opened it to the middle section. "Elementary psychology teaches us that everyone wants to feel important. Everyone wants approval. It's easier to win friends by being interested in others than by trying to get them interested in us. Using these premises as a base, I suggest that we direct our interest toward our many planters. I suggest that we salute them individually in our newspaper advertising."

Alex impressed Jess. His mind was as neatly organized as his desk. His idea was not a mere shot in the dark; he could back it up with facts.

"In what way do you plan to salute these people?" Mr. Wong asked.

"On the days when we run a full-page advertisement, I think it would be a good idea to feature one planter. Let him be the outstanding thing on that page. We could tell a bit about him and about his fields. I haven't worked out details yet. But this would tell each planter that we think of him personally."

"Sounds good." Mr. Wong rolled a pencil between his palms. "Anything else?"

"Yes. I think the company paper might print a brief biography of each worker. We might devote a whole column to this and use the employee's picture to head it."

"That's been done a thousand times," Johnny argued as he propped his sandaled feet on his desk top. "That's no new idea."

"It hasn't been done a thousand times with this group of employees," Mr. Wong snapped. "What better idea can you offer?"

"There was nothing in my agreement with you or with the university that said I had to be an idea man," Johnny replied. "I'm just here to edit your paper. And that I do."

"In that case please refrain from entering

this discussion." Mr. Wong rose and paced the office, and Johnny busied himself by bringing his scrapbook up to date, by inserting the latest issues of *Pine Pack News* between specially designed clear plastic sheets.

Reeta was batting her eyelashes at Alex when Mr. Wong asked for her ideas.

"I've been thinking that we should do something along the cultural line." Reeta looked away from Jess. "We must appeal to the whole community, you know. I think it would be a good plan to sponsor the Honolulu symphony in a series of concerts."

Jess felt her mouth fall open, then she clenched her fists so tightly that the pencil in her hand snapped in two. Was Reeta serious? How could she have the gall to repeat the idea Jess had told her only minutes ago?

"Be patient, Jess," her dad said. "We'll get to you in just a minute."

Jess jerked her desk drawer open and fumbled for a fresh pencil. She was tempted to make a scene over Reeta's unfairness, but some inner voice compelled her to silence. Now what should she do? Reeta's mean trick left her with exactly no idea to present to the group. Her dad would think she was a complete flop. Jess could hardly bear that thought, nor could she stomach the approval stamped on Alex's face as he smiled at Reeta.

"Anything else, Reeta?" Mr. Wong asked.

"Yes. I think Pine Pack might use a give-away of some sort. I had in mind a small folder of recipes using pineapple. Perhaps we could ask some prominent and well-known Honolulu ladies to contribute their favorite recipes."

Mr. Wong nodded and paused while his secretary made a note of the idea. Jess's mind wandered from Reeta's words and she jumped with a start as she heard her father call her name.

"Now, Jess. What have you thought of?"

A moment ago Jess's mind had been blank, but now she had an idea that seemed to come to her full blown. Yet she knew it hadn't come all of a piece. It had come in bits and snatches, and her mind had somehow glued the fragments together.

"Dad, you told me on my first night in Hawaii that you respected the person who thought differently. Those words stuck in my mind. A while back Johnny and I saw a little girl on the beach who thought differently. I remember her well. While the other kids clutched their helium-filled balloons, she deliberately released hers because she wanted to write a story about it. Soon her friends had forgotten about their own balloons. They were begging to hear her tale."

"What's all that have to do with Pine Pack?" Reeta asked.

"The girl brought to my attention the fact that children love stories," Jess said. "I think we could win goodwill from our consumers on the mainland by giving them a booklet containing a Hawaiian folktale when they purchase a Pine Pack product. We could even have a series of folktales. This might appeal to the childrens' collector instinct."

"I already thought of the giveaway idea," Reeta said.

"But this one is different," Alex said. "It's unique as far as I know. Lots of companies publish recipes."

Jess flashed Alex a glance of thanks and avoided looking at Reeta. Why didn't her father speak? What was he thinking?

"Jess, who would write the folktales?" Mr. Wong asked.

"I think I could, Dad. I've had some creative writing training in my quest for a teaching degree. I could do some research and come up with some authentic tales."

"Won't copyright laws prevent you from stealing such material?" Reeta emphasized the word stealing.

"Folktales, if they are authentic, usually

date back to antiquity," Jess said. "Such material is in the public domain. Of course, I would retell the tales in a vocabulary children would enjoy."

"Mr. Wong." Reeta stood. "I object. It makes more sense to appeal to adults — they control the family spending. Recipes are an adult thing."

"I feel that both ideas are good; but what do you think of Reeta's criticism, Jess?"

"It's certainly true that adults control family spending, but they'll spend for what their kids want. The educational value of a folktale pamphlet will appeal to mothers. Its entertainment value will appeal to the kids. And even grandmas and grandpas will enjoy something they can read aloud to the smallfry. Our company would be promoting Hawaii and Pine Pack Pineapple at the same time. I submit the idea also as appealing to the community."

For several moments nobody spoke. Reeta's creamy complexion was flushed to an angry pink, and Johnny gazed at Reeta, then winked broadly at Jess. Alex stared out the window, deep in thought, while Mr. Wong scribbled numbers on a clipboard that he propped on his knee.

"Recipes or folktales," he began, "any giveaway is going to be expensive. It's hard to say which idea will have more appeal without actually trying both of them."

"Why not do just that?" Alex broke in. "We could try both ideas on a limited basis here on Oahu. When we learn which idea has the most appeal, we can launch the mainland campaign."

"Good thinking, Alex." Mr. Wong jumped to his feet and clapped Alex on the back. "That's exactly what we'll do. Reeta, do you think you can get the recipes?"

"Of course, Mr. Wong. I have connections with all the best families in Honolulu."

"And you, Jess. How soon can you have a group of folktales for us to choose from?"

"May I have a week or two?" Jess asked.

"That seems reasonable enough. The general office work must go on. These extra projects will have to be sandwiched in. While we're waiting for the recipes and the folktales, I believe I'll go ahead and contact the symphony business manager about a concert series. And Alex, you proceed with developing ideas for the biographies and the pictures of planters and cannery personnel.

"But hear this. Everything we've said in this room today is top secret. In the past some of our PR ideas have leaked to competitors. I don't want that to happen again. Don't discuss these ideas outside of this office."

"I'll have to tell the ladies why I want their recipes," Reeta said.

"Be vague," Alex advised. "Just say we want them for use in our advertising. Don't elaborate."

"I'll pretend to be collecting folktales for my own personal enjoyment," Jess said.

"Fine." Mr. Wong headed for the door. "I'll check with this office from time to time to keep a line on what's happening. Now back to the day's routine."

Once Mr. Wong left the office, the usual casual atmosphere returned. Jess was discussing folktales with Johnny, unmindful of the time, when Reeta interrupted.

"If you can tear yourself away from our editor, Jess, the mail is waiting for your undivided attention."

The mail. Jess had forgotten all about regular assignments in her excitement over coming up with an idea that pleased her father. She had dismissed Reeta's treachery from her mind, and when she realized that she had had a good idea, a feeling she could hardly describe buoyed her. It was a sense of accomplishment, a sense of having touched the lives of others, a sense of being a vital part of an important company.

Jess grabbed the stack of mail and began sorting it. She placed Alex's and Reeta's personal mail in their in baskets, then she opened the general mail. One envelope contained clippings, which she filed in the clipping box. Another folder contained carbons of letters to be routed within the company offices. Two trade papers blared black headlines. A memo from her father requested that employees arrive at work on time. Jess made a mental note to write the memo in correct form and circulate it throughout the cannery to all personnel.

The last letter Jess picked up bore her own name, and a swift glance at the return address told her that it was from Superintendent Higgins. Jess thrust the unopened letter into her purse, but in a few moments curiosity got the better of her and she ripped the envelope open and spread the message out on her desk.

Seaside School
November 10

Miss Jessica Wong
Pine Pack Inc.
Honolulu, Hawaii

Dear Miss Wong:

This letter is to advise you that our

school will be in need of a third grade teacher who is willing to fill out the school term beginning in December. If you are still interested in such an opportunity, please contact me at your earliest convenience.

Respectfully,
R. R. Higgins, Supt. of Schools

Jess stuffed the letter into her purse and sighed. Two months ago she would have jumped at the chance to teach, but now, just this morning, her attitude had changed completely. She was torn between wanting to teach and wanting to see her PR idea through to completion.

Chapter Ten

That evening after dinner Mr. Wong went back to his downtown office to work, and Jess, Ora, and Malia sat on the lanai visiting. Malia began stringing a lei to wear on her date that evening, but once Ora went to the kitchen Malia questioned Jess.

"What did Dad say when you suggested sponsoring a concert series?"

Jess inhaled the scent of the plumeria blossoms and sighed. "He liked the idea, but it came from Reeta, not from me."

"How did that happen?" Malia asked. "Had Reeta thought of the same idea?"

"I don't know. I suppose I pulled a stupid trick. I discussed the idea with her before the meeting, then when Dad asked Reeta for her contribution, she gave him that one."

"And you just sat there!" Malia dropped her lei string, and three blossoms slipped onto the flagged lanai.

"I was too stunned to protest," Jess said. "And it's a good thing that I was. How would it have looked if I had made a fuss? I would have put Dad in the position of having to choose which one of us was telling the truth. And if he chose me, it would have looked like favoritism to the others. I guess it really doesn't matter where the idea originated as long as it helps Pine Pack."

"That Reeta!" Malia jumped as she pricked her thumb with her needle. "She comes on like Snow White, but all the time she's planning something sneaky. I think she's jealous of you, Jess. She's probably trying to get even with you for going out with Alex."

"I doubt that. She could see that we were discussing business. That would hardly inspire jealousy."

Malia snorted. "Reeta would probably trade her false eyelashes for a date with Alex whether they discussed business or pleasure."

Malia finished her lei just as her date arrived. Jess helped her slip it over her head, then watched her ride off into the soft tropic evening with a handsome young man in a blue convertible.

With her dad and Malia away, the house seemed almost deserted. Jess heard a radio playing in some distant wing as she stepped into the living room to check the bookshelves. Would the Wongs have any volumes of folktales? Jess searched thoroughly, but she found only one thin book that she could use.

Taking the book to her room, Jess prepared for bed, then she read until she fell asleep. The book was still lying by her side when she awakened the next morning, and before she left for work she tucked it into her handbag. She might find some time at the office to study it further.

Johnny, Alex, and Reeta were all at their desks when Jess stepped into the PR office. After a brief exchange of alohas she checked her daily calendar for chores to be done, then busied herself sorting the mail. She was clipping tear sheets on a news story that had appeared the previous day when her father stepped into the office.

"Jess." He strode to her desk. "How about coming with me for an hour or so? I'm going to present the concert series idea to Mr. Sanford, the business manager of the symphony. It'll be good experience for you to sit in on the session."

"Jess has quite a few routine chores to do this morning," Reeta said, smiling at Mr. Wong. "Perhaps I should go with you instead." Reeta turned a wide-eyed gaze on her boss and leaned forward just enough to cause her hair to cascade over her shoulder in a silvery mass.

"Afraid not, Reeta." Mr. Wong grinned. "I know this was your idea, but that's the very reason Jess should go. You're too close to the situation. I don't want Mr. Sanford to feel any tension, and I do want Jess to have the experience of sitting in on an important interview. We should be back by mid-morning. In the meantime you can take care of the routine chores. I always feel confident when you're on the job."

Jess could hardly keep from smiling as phrases such as poetic justice floated through her mind. She grabbed her purse and followed her father from the office and into the waiting car before Reeta could think up some other excuse to keep her at her desk.

"Do you want me to take notes or anything, Dad? My shorthand's strictly of the high school variety, but . . ."

"That won't be necessary, Jess." Mr. Wong eased the car through the morning traffic. "Just keep your eyes and ears open. You may be in charge of this sort of interview some day in the future."

Mr. Sanford's office was near the orchestra rehearsal hall, and as they entered the building Jess heard the muted sound of violins and cellos. Somewhere a harpist

139

plucked an arpeggio, and from a far distance she heard a pianist thumping out scales. Mr. Sanford's secretary greeted them, and after a short wait in an outer office appointed with orchids and anthuriums she admitted them to Mr. Sanford's private office.

Jess shook hands with Mr. Sanford and smiled a greeting, but as soon as her dad began speaking, her eyes wandered to the office walls, which were almost covered with autographed photos of musicians. In the photographs men in tuxedos held French horns and trumpets. Ladies in flowing evening gowns were pictured with violas, flutes, or clarinets.

"Pine Pack would like to sponsor a series of symphony concerts, pick up the entire tab." Mr. Wong paused and cleared his throat. "It could be a special adult series or even a children's series. I'd want you to be the judge of what's best."

Mr. Sanford remained silent for what seemed like a long moment, then he shook his head. "How strange that you should call on me today with this proposal."

"Why so strange?" Mr. Wong ran his fingers through his dark hair.

Mr. Sanford sighed and looked at a spot to the left of Mr. Wong. "Strange because Mr. Brietag of Commercial Can called on me only yesterday with a similar proposal. Of course I accepted. I couldn't afford to do otherwise. But I can hardly accept two such similar offers. I hope you understand my position."

"I understand perfectly, Mr. Sanford." Mr. Wong rose and shook hands with Mr. Sanford. "Perhaps we can get together on some arrangements at a later date. I'll keep it in mind."

"Thank you for coming by," Mr. Sanford said. "I appreciate your interest. The symphony needs dedicated backers."

Jess admired the professional way her dad handled his disappointment. Calm. Cool. Efficient. At least that's the way he appeared in the practice hall. But once he was in the privacy of his own car, he exploded in anger and indignation.

"This raw deal can't be coincidence, Jess. I'm no fool. Someone has leaked secret information again, and I'll bet it was Reeta McQuigg. This plan was her idea. Either intentionally or accidentally she talked of it to someone who snatched it up for Brietag."

"Don't be too quick to blame Reeta," Jess warned. "I guess I'd better tell you that the symphony idea wasn't really hers."

"Was it yours?" Mr. Wong stared at Jess

so intently that he almost swerved into a parked car.

"It was Malia's plan," Jess said. "When I could think of no ideas to present, she suggested it to me. I made the mistake of mentioning it to Reeta before the meeting, and she sort of picked up on it."

"But why didn't you tell me?"

"Dad! How would that have looked? I would have forced you into an embarrassing position. Anyway, perhaps it was better for the idea to come from Reeta. If it came from me, the others might think you went along with it just to help Malia, who's vitally concerned with the symphony."

"All the same I wish I had known sooner."

"What are you going to do now?" Jess asked as they pulled into the Pine Pack parking lot.

"We're going back into the PR office," Mr. Wong said. "You'll enter first. It's not time for coffee break yet, so everyone should be there. I'll tell them exactly what happened, and we'll both watch each of them for reactions. If any one of them is guilty, surely he'll give himself away by some look or word or mannerism."

A chill prickled along the nape of Jess's neck. She could hardly be a neutral observer when she felt such a strong dislike for Reeta and when she felt so fond of Johnny and Alex. But she said nothing. She watched her father arrange a noncommital expression on his face as they entered the PR room.

"How did it go?" Reeta stood and stepped forward. Johnny and Alex looked up with interest, but neither rose from his desk.

"Commercial Can got the scoop on us," Mr. Wong said slowly. "It seems that their representative called on Mr. Sanford yesterday and made a deal with him to sponsor a concert series. What do you think of that!"

"Impossible!" Reeta exclaimed. "It can't be coincidence, Mr. Wong. It simply can't."

"I agree completely," Mr. Wong said. "And I intend to find out who's responsible for the information leak. Make no mistake about that. I intend to find out."

Jess watched her father turn on his heel and stride from the room. She was still thinking about the reactions of the others when Reeta flared at her.

"You leaked the information, didn't you, Jess?" Reeta pounded her fist on Jess's desk. "You did it because you were mad at me. You weren't going to let me take credit for a good idea, were you? You were boiling mad because I . . ."

"Because you what?" Alex stepped to Jess's desk. "Because you preempted Jess's idea? Is that what you were going to say?"

"Of course it wasn't," Reeta snapped. "I have enough ideas of my own. I don't have to stoop to using anyone else's."

"How convenient that you're dating Bruce Brietag," Alex said. "I wonder if Mr. Wong knows that you're seeing the son of his competitor on a social basis. Or is it purely social?"

"I'll date whomever I please." Reeta spat the words. "My social life is none of your affair."

"You'd better drop Bruce Brietag or you'll be hunting a new job."

"How dare you threaten me!" Reeta glared at Alex then flounced from the room.

"Alex!" Jess said when Reeta was gone. "Can you — would you really fire Reeta because of her personal life?"

Alex shook his head. "I'm sorry. I lost my temper. If there's anything I can't stand it's a cheat and a sneak. I think Reeta's the one who's giving away our ideas. She's just trying to cover her tracks by accusing you."

Jess gulped. It pleased and flattered her to have Alex as an ally, but it also frightened her. Reeta was her immediate superior; she had to get along with Reeta if she continued working at Pine Pack. Alex's rash accusation could trigger lots of trouble.

"Why pick on Reeta?" Johnny stood, stretched, and yawned. An orchid blossom fell from behind his ear, and he stooped to retrieve it. "I'm the guy with the motive. You all know that I hate big business. Why aren't you putting me on the spot? It would be much more logical than accusing Reeta."

Jess listened to the dialogue with mounting horror. What was happening here? Everyone was saying things he would regret.

"You have no logical reason to give away ideas." Alex glared at Johnny. "You may hate big business, but you'd hardly bother to undermine one business just in order to help another. That makes no sense."

"Let's all get back to work," Jess said. "Let's get on with the routine of the day. We are not judge and jury."

"Right, Jess." Reeta spoke from the doorway which she had entered unnoticed. "Let's all get back to work. This is Mr. Wong's problem."

Jess performed her routine chores automatically. But try as she might to forget it, the problem of finding the informer nagged at her. She had been all too willing to suspect Reeta until Alex had made such a scene. It was unlike him to speak out so bluntly. Could he be blaming Reeta in an attempt to divert suspicion from himself?

Jess skipped her coffee break in order to catch up on the jobs that had accumulated while she was out of the office. She even worked during part of her lunch hour although Johnny had invited her to eat at the Surfside with him, a treat she usually thoroughly enjoyed. By early afternoon her desk was clear and she pulled the book of folktales from her purse and began studying them, trying to decide which one might be most appealing to children.

"If you're all caught up," Reeta said, "I have some things you can do."

"I'm working on my folktale project," Jess explained.

"Well, that's just reading. You can do that anytime. Here. I want you to call these ladies and ask them for their pineapple recipes. As Alex says, be vague. Just ask if they have one that we might use in our advertising. Make it sound as if we're doing them a favor if you can. Emphasize that their name will be published."

Jess wanted to shout at the unfairness of Reeta's request, but there had been enough shouting in the office for one day. She took the list of numbers Reeta held out and pulled the telephone closer to her. She dialed the first number.

"Mrs. Hoskin speaking," a voice sang over the wire.

"Mrs. Hoskin, this is Miss Jess Wong calling from the office of Pine Pack. We're seeking pineapple recipes to use in our advertising, and we are wondering if you have one you would care to share with us."

Jess listened to the hum of the telephone connection for a few moments, then Mrs. Hoskin answered her.

"Why, yes, I do have some delicious recipes that require pineapple as an important ingredient. One especially good one has been passed down to me from my mother, who received it from her mother. It's been in the family for at least three generations. I would be happy for you to use it as long as you list our family as your source."

"Of course we would want to do that," Jess replied. "Do you have time to give me the recipe now?"

"Oh, I'd never trust repeating it over the telephone," Mrs. Hoskin said.

"If you'd rather mail it to me, that would be fine," Jess suggested.

"I would prefer that you call personally for it," Mrs. Hoskin said. "Would that be possible? I'll be home all afternoon."

"Of course," Jess said. "I have your address here, and either I or Miss McQuigg will call upon you within the hour. Thank you very much."

Jess replaced the receiver in its cradle and looked at Reeta. "You heard. She wants someone to pick up the recipe in person. Do you want to go?"

"Of course not," Reeta said. "You're the junior around here. You do the legwork." Reeta glanced at her watch. "You should be able to make it out there and back within an hour if you get started right away. Better check with your dad about taking the company car."

Jess rose and picked up her purse, but before she could leave the office Alex called to her.

"Your dad's out in the company car, Jess, and there's no point in taking a taxi. I'll drive you in my car. I have another errand out that way."

"I've changed my mind," Reeta said. "I'll go after all."

"Not on your life, Reeta." Alex glared at her. "I just dropped a lot of work onto your in basket. I'm sure you'll be busy until quitting time. Come on, Jess. Let's go."

Jess followed Alex from the office with mixed emotions. She liked to be with him. If it weren't for Malia's interest in him, she might even fall for him in a big way. But she hated leaving Reeta in a rage. Everybody's temper was on a short leash today, and she hated to be responsible for another outburst from Reeta. But Alex was PR boss; she went along with him.

Chapter Eleven

Alex took the beach drive to Mrs. Hoskin's house, and Jess relaxed for the first time that day. Sea and sky, the windswept sand, and the pandanus trees with their soft, feather-duster leaves all had a soothing effect on her. She tried to imagine that she and Alex were off for a pleasure excursion.

"Did you really have another errand out this way?" Jess asked.

"What do you think?" Alex grinned. "You don't seem to understand that I enjoy being with you, and you've turned me down the last two times I've asked you out. I have a feeling that Johnny Kuhio is really beating my time."

"I enjoy Johnny's company," Jess said. "You'll have to admit that he's charming."

"Oh, that he is. Beach boys get lots of practice. Lots of practice at being charming. All the girls like Johnny Kuhio."

"You don't do too badly on the charm practice either," Jess said. "I've noticed that little book you carry in your pocket."

"I just have a few names to fall back on

when you've turned me down."

"What a line!" Jess laughed. She liked Alex, but at the same time Johnny was on her mind. Alex talked constantly, and she missed the silences she shared with Johnny, silences when each seemed to know what the other was thinking without any words passing between them.

Alex was trying to talk her into going out with him that night when they arrived at the Hoskin mansion.

"What a place!" Jess studied the house with its turrets and cupolas. "I was expecting something more Hawaiian modern. This looks like a home right out of old New England."

"It's a leftover from the ancient days when the missionaries arrived in the islands, bringing their ideas on religion as well as on architecture." Alex stopped the car in front of the main entryway. "I'll wait here for you."

"Why don't you come in with me? I'm not scared, but you would lend dignity and importance to the occasion. Evidently parting with a recipe is a big deal for Mrs. Hoskin."

Alex slipped from the car and they both walked to the door. To Jess's surprise Mrs. Hoskin was waiting for them.

"You're the people from Pine Pack?" she

asked, fluttering a handkerchief which wafted jasmine scent into the air.

"Yes, ma'am. I'm Jess Wong and this is my boss, Mr. Yanagisako. It's most generous of you to let us use your recipe. We appreciate it."

Mrs. Hoskin led them through a spacious living room to cushioned chairs on a veranda. A high hibiscus hedge separated the Hoskin yard from neighboring yards, and banana and papaya trees dotted the well-manicured lawn.

Mrs. Hoskin rang a silver bell, and in a moment an Oriental girl appeared bearing a recipe card upon a silver tray. Mrs. Hoskin picked up the card and dismissed the girl.

"Lelani has copied the recipe for me, and I am proud to present it to you." Mrs. Hoskin tucked the recipe card into an envelope and handed it to Jess. "Do you have time to stay for tea?"

"Thank you, but I'm afraid we haven't," Alex spoke up. "We're due back at the office within the hour. We do appreciate your generosity. You will be hearing from Mr. Wong soon."

Mrs. Hoskin rose and ushered them back to the front doorway, where Jess expressed her thanks before they departed.

"She was nice, wasn't she?" Jess asked

when they were again driving down the beach road.

"Oh, yes indeed. Our Reeta knows all the right people."

"Can't you forget Reeta for a while?" Jess asked. "You've really let her upset you."

"I'll forget her if you'll promise to go out with me tonight. How about it?"

"I really can't, Alex. I'd like to, but I simply can't. If I'm going to have to do the legwork and the telephoning for the recipe brochure, that means I'll have to do the research for my folktales on my own time. But I'm willing to do that. I believe in that idea, and I'll not let it fall by the wayside. Tonight I'll be haunting some library. That's the way it has to be."

Alex stopped at a drive-in and bought them both coconut malts to go, then he drove to a quiet cove while they drank them.

"Best coffee break I've had all week," he said, letting his hand fall over Jess's.

Jess felt her heart thump madly, and she hoped Alex couldn't hear it. She was on the verge of relenting, of agreeing to go out with him, when she remembered the letter from Mr. Higgins. She sighed, and as she sighed Alex leaned over and kissed her tenderly. To her surprise she found herself responding to the kiss. In that moment she knew she and Alex were no longer merely business associates, co-workers. She knew and Alex knew.

"Alex, we'd better get back to the office," Jess said. "It's getting late."

"I'll go back," Alex said. "But I'm driving you on home. Take the rest of the afternoon to work on your stories. Reeta and I will cover the office chores."

Jess felt that she should protest, but she couldn't bring herself to do it. She could use an hour or two alone after all that had gone on today. She accepted Alex's offer, but before she left the car she handed him the envelope containing the recipe.

"Better give it to Reeta, so she'll know I really was working. And thanks so much for all the help."

Alex smiled and drove off toward Pine Pack.

Once in her room, Jess paced until she realized that she was copying her father's mannerism. She flopped down on the bed and did some straight thinking. She wanted to teach school. Public relations work interested her, but it soared her to ecstasy only to plunge her to the depths of despair. Just thinking of the ugly scene that had taken place in the office that morning put Jess in the mood to write her letter of resignation.

Tomorrow she must contact Mr. Higgins. There was still time, and she was glad of that. The days between now and December would give her the opportunity to make a proper exit from Pine Pack. It occurred to her that there was a right way and a wrong way to leave a company.

Jess realized that just because she was resigning from her job she was in no position of superiority. She had no right to do entirely as she pleased when it came to leaving Pine Pack. She must resign properly. She would tidy up her records and help make an orderly transition possible. Perhaps her dad would want to hire a successor immediately so Jess could help train her.

Jess scowled. Of course she would have to hand her resignation to Reeta even though the temptation was great to bypass her immediate superior and give the resignation to Alex or even to her father. She sighed. By giving her letter directly to Reeta she would be retaining participation as a team member until her last day of employment.

Jess was still composing her resignation letter when the telephone rang and Johnny's voice flowed over the wire.

"How about we go out tonight and watch the submarine races?"

"What submarine races?" Jess asked. "I

hadn't heard of them."

"Sometimes they're hard to see," Johnny admitted, "but nothing can stop us from going to watch."

Jess caught the joking tone in Johnny's voice and laughed at herself for being so gullible. "Can't make it tonight, Johnny. Sorry. I absolutely have to stay home and work on that booklet I suggested at the big meeting."

"How can you work on it at home?" Johnny asked. "I had nothing special in mind to do tonight. Come with me and I'll take you to the university library. You can find some authentic Hawaiian stories there. Then we could walk to Waikiki and talk to Naniloa."

"Naniloa? Who's that?"

"A very old lady who runs the lei stand on the beach. I know she could probably give you some authentic tales for your collection."

"It's a date, Johnny. You're a doll to think of it."

"Pick you up at six-thirty," Johnny said. "We'll have supper at International Market Place and work from there."

"Fine. See you then."

Jess hid her letter of resignation in her desk drawer where nobody was likely to see it. She had worked on it longer than she had realized. She would have to hurry to be ready by six-thirty.

Johnny called for her promptly, and Jess grinned up at him as he helped her into the jeep. People stared as they passed by, making Jess feel like a tourist. At International Market Place they ate at the Cock's Roost, an upstairs restaurant where charbroiled steaks were a speciality of the house. Jess wished that they could just relax and spend the whole evening there, but she knew that could not be.

After they finished eating Johnny led her to an area where people were crowding onto green benches that were arranged in front of an outdoor stage. Jess hung back, but Johnny urged her to a seat.

"There'll be a Polynesian show here in a few minutes." Johnny glanced at his watch. "It's worth seeing, Jess. It might give you some background material for your folktales. I'll speed you to the library just as soon as the show ends. That's a promise."

Jess didn't argue, and in a matter of minutes all the seats around them were filled and a strange wailing keened from behind the crowd.

"The sounding of the conch," Johnny explained.

Presently Jess saw a boy clad only in a red hip sarong walk down the center aisle between the benches. He held a huge conch shell to his lips, blowing into it to produce the eerie wailing. A succession of dancers followed him onto the stage.

Jess watched the program in fascination. Beautiful Oriental girls told stories in song and dance, using graceful movements of hips, arms and hands. A Polynesian boy performed a fast dance, using a flaming sword. At the end of his number he sliced a fresh pineapple with the sword and tossed the juicy morsels into the crowd.

"No doubt it was a Pine Pack fruit," Jess said with a laugh.

"Great idea," Johnny said. "You should tell your dad to see that the boy uses only fruit with the Pine Pack trademark."

After they left the Polynesian show, open-front shops featuring black coral, Pele's tears, jade, and souveniers tempted Jess to stop and browse, but she was firm in her insistence that they go directly to the library. Johnny drove to the university, showed his student's pass to an official, then drove onto the campus. He parked the jeep, and they walked to the library.

"I wish I was quick at using the card catalogue." Jess sniffed the stuffy odor of the library. "I'm afraid the stacks will close before I find what I want."

"Forget the card catalogue," Johnny advised. "I know the girl at the desk. She'll find what you want on the double."

Jess had her doubts, but after Johnny explained what type of book Jess needed, the girl called a page, and together they disappeared into the stacks. In a matter of moments they returned with five books containing Hawaiian history and folklore.

"Thank you so much," Jess said to the librarian. "I really appreciate your help."

"You should be able to find something you can use in all that material," Johnny said as they walked to the jeep. "But it will take hours of reading just to sort out what you can use and what you can't."

"Johnny, I really appreciate your help. I could have searched for weeks without finding this much information."

"Don't forget, the best is yet to come. You still have to meet Naniloa. Let's head for her stand right now."

Jess enjoyed the feel of the evening breeze against her cheeks as they drove toward the beach. The smell of the sea was all about them, and she imagined that she could taste the salt spray in the air as they parked the jeep and walked toward a small bamboo stand across from a souvenier shop.

"Naniloa," Johnny said, smiling at the old lady in charge, "I want you to meet a friend of mine. This is Jess Wong."

Jess tried not to stare at the huge proportions of the woman squeezed inside the lei booth. "I'm glad to know you, Naniloa. Johnny's brought me here to ask a favor of you. You see, I'm collecting Hawaiian folktales, and he thought you might know some very special ones."

Naniloa nodded and continued stringing lavender orchids onto a thread. All around her strings of blossoms hung from nails on the wall of her stand, and the scent of jasmine and carnation sweetened the air.

"You want to hear tales of how the god Maui held the sun on his shoulders until his island was drawn from the depths of the ocean? Or you want to hear about the menehuenes on the island of Kauai? I know those tales."

"I would love to hear them," Jess said. "But you are too busy to talk with me now."

Naniloa nodded in agreement. "But tomorrow at my house I am willing to talk to any of Johnny's friends. Can you come then?"

"Of course you can," Johnny said as Jess hesitated. "It's Saturday. We'll go in the morning before I go to work. Okay?"

"It's fine with me if it suits Naniloa," Jess said.

Johnny made the arrangements. As they stood at the lei booth visiting with Naniloa, Jess saw Alex strolling along the beach with a pretty Oriental girl at his side. Jess tried to step out of sight until they passed, but it was impossible. Alex not only saw her with Johnny, but he waved to them.

What would Alex think! After refusing a date with him, it was almost unforgivable for her to be seen out with another man. Of course, she might be able to explain, but it embarrassed her to think of it.

Jess glanced from Alex's departing figure back to Johnny. How could she be so fascinated by two men at the same time? Perhaps the reason was because they were such opposites. Yes. That must be it.

"It's been a wonderful evening, Johnny," Jess said as they strolled back toward the jeep. "You have a knack for turning simple events into major attractions."

"I'm glad you've noticed." Johnny drove for a while, then he parked the jeep beneath a palm tree and they sat watching the moon shimmer on the sea and listening to the waves washing onto the sand. Jess wished that she could stop time and hold this moment forever, but before she became completely carried away by the beauty of the tropical evening combined with Johnny's soothing voice and winning ways, she insisted on going home.

"I'll pick you up in the morning," Johnny promised as he walked with Jess to her door. "Can you be ready by nine? It's a ways into the mountain valley to Naniloa's home."

"I'll be ready," Jess promised.

Brushing Jess's cheek with a kiss, Johnny left her on her doorstep.

Chapter Twelve

Malia was out on a date, and Jess spent the remainder of the evening reading and studying the books she had borrowed. But no matter how hard she tried to concentrate, Johnny's face kept appearing in her mind's eye as she read about Pele the Fire Goddess and Kane the creator of all life.

When at last Jess turned out her light, she still couldn't get to sleep. The Hawaiian tales fascinated her, and so did Johnny. She admired his determination to get an excellent education, and she also admired his quick intellect that would make it possible for him to succeed at whatever he put his mind to. Only his image of himself as a displaced person bothered her.

Jess couldn't believe that Johnny's was the sort of different thinking that her father professed to admire. And his job as a beach boy at the Surfside bothered her. With a doctorate degree almost within his grasp, he seemed content to lie for hours on the beach and to play endlessly in the sand and surf. Johnny was an enigma.

The next morning Jess dressed casually in slacks and a sport shirt, and she tossed a red and white gingham head scarf in her purse to protect her hair on the ride to the valley. Her father was off on a business trip, and Malia was already in her studio teaching by the time Jess stepped into the dining room, so she ate alone. She had barely finished her cereal when she heard Johnny's jeep in the driveway.

"Aloha," Jess called as Johnny strolled up the front sidewalk. "What a lovely day! I'm glad we're going to the valley."

"Every day's a beautiful day when I'm with you," Johnny said, smiling.

"I'll bet you say that to all the girls." Jess laughed as she climbed into the jeep, and Johnny didn't deny her accusation. The sun glinted on the frothing surf as they drove beside the sea, but when they turned toward the mountains, black clouds mounded in the sky. Lightning flashed above the tropical forest, and in moments rain began pelting on the canvas jeep top.

"Wow!" Jess eased closer to Johnny. "Guess I should have brought an umbrella."

"No need. It never rains very long. Really, if you'd stop to check, you'd probably find that it's pineapple juice coming down."

Johnny was right about the rain's duration. Before they reached a small sign that marked the winding lane to Naniloa's home, the shower had stopped, and a rainbow arched across the sky.

"That's a good luck omen." Jess peered at the rainbow. "It means that Naniloa will tell me a super-keen folktale that'll be a smash hit with all the pineapple-eating small fry on the mainland."

Johnny parked the jeep in front of a small frame house that was little more than a cabin. A banyan tree shaded it from the sun, and pandanus trees with their ariel roots shooting obliquely from their trunks formed a sort of windbreak behind the structure. Their jeep had no more than stopped when Naniloa appeared in the cabin doorway, filling it from frame to frame. She wore a bright yellow muumuu, and she reminded Jess of a life-size balloon.

"Aloha, Naniloa," Johnny called.

"Aloha, Johnny and Jess. I have spent the early morning hours thinking of tales to tell you, and I've brewed some tea to enjoy while we visit. Please come in and sit down."

Jess stepped through the doorway onto a woven-rush floor mat and took a chair at the table Naniloa motioned toward. The house and its furnishings seemed small in comparison to the gigantic proportions of its owner, but everything was spotlessly clean, and the chairs drawn up to the table glowed with a special sheen. Jess rubbed her forefinger along the arm of her chair.

"What beautiful wood. It's quite unusual."

"It is the koa wood. My father bring it down from the mountains many years ago. He made the chairs you see here. My grandfather also bring koa logs from the mountain, but he no made furniture. He hollowed the logs into canoes."

"Your father was an excellent craftsman," Jess said. "Each chair is a piece of art." Jess glanced around the room while Johnny folded his long legs beneath the table. The plain muslin curtains at the windows gave the room a light, airy look, and Jess guessed that the room served as both a dining and sitting area. Before Naniloa joined them at the table she served hot tea and pineapple spears, then she picked up some handwork she was fashioning and sat down beside Jess.

"What are you making?" Jess asked.

"I'm weaving a basket of pandanus leaves." Naniloa held the project toward Jess. "It occupies my hands while my mind wanders free."

Jess touched the stiff fibers in the part of the basket that was completed. "It's lovely and distinctive. How long does it take you to weave such a basket?"

"The weaving never takes so very long. The preparation of the fibers is the big thing. First I dry the leaves in the sun, then I bleach them in salt water and scrape them until they're smooth. When I've cut them in long narrow strips like the ones you see here, they are ready for weaving."

Jess sipped her tea and inhaled the mingled odors of dried pandanus fibers and fresh pineapple as Naniloa spoke again.

"I have thought about many tales that my grandmother used to tell me. There is one about a pearl. Another about a porpoise. Still another about the City of Refuge. Which one would you like to hear first?"

"The one about the porpoise," Jess said, choosing at random. "It sounds as if it catches the flavor of the islands. I've brought a steno's pad and ballpoint with me. I hope you won't mind if I record your tale."

"Not at all," Naniloa said. "Just do not interrupt me. My mind cannot hold the tale if there are interruptions."

"I won't say a word," Jess promised. "I'm ready whenever you care to begin."

Naniloa cleared her throat. "The name of the tale is *Pekea The Porpoise.*

On a coral reef carved by the sea, Moki played with his pet porpoise, Pekea. The moon had waxed and waned many times since Moki and Pekea first met; there was understanding between them.

Pekea the Porpoise taught Moki to glide through the sea faster than any other boy on the island of Niihau. In turn Moki taught his pet to leap, to turn somersaults in the air, and to dance on his tail. One day while Moki and Pekea were playing in the waves, Moki's sister, Lelani, rushed into the surf.

"Moki!" she called. "A stranger visits our village."

Moki swam to Lelani's side. "A stranger? Why does this excite you so?"

"I have come to warn you," Lelani said. "The stranger carries a pearl-edged harpoon. He seeks Pekea the Porpoise."

Although the sun shone brightly, Moki shivered as he splashed ashore. "I will run to the village," he said. "I must tell this stranger that Pekea is my pet."

By the time Moki and Lelani arrived in the village, a great crowd had gathered around the stranger called Akamai. From the words being spoken Moki knew it was useless to claim Pekea as his pet. The stranger was not the kind who would understand.

"I must have the great porpoise," Akamai said to the crowd. "By sunset tomorrow I must pay taxes to our king. I have grown nothing. I have no crops to offer, yet I believe the king will like the gift of a great porpoise."

The villagers knew Pekea the Porpoise was Moki's friend; they told this to the stranger. When he paid no attention to them, they made up tales to frighten him away.

"You must never harpoon the great porpoise," one man said. "This fish has an evil spirit. Bad luck will follow one who harms him."

"I am not afraid," Akamai said. "I must have that fish."

"Leave him alone," a woman cried. "He belongs in Niihau waters."

Akamai sneered. "By tomorrow he will be mine. Where may I spend the night?"

No one answered, and at last Moki inched forward. "Akamai, you may stay at my home. Come, we will go there now."

"Why do you invite your enemy into our home?" Lelani whispered.

"With Akamai near, I will know his plans," Moki replied. "Perhaps I will think of a way to protect Pekea."

"But Akamai has watched Pekea on the reef," Lelani said. "He knows that the porpoise appears each morning. Pekea will be no match for one with a pearl-edged harpoon."

"Hush, Lelani," Moki said. "He comes."

That evening Moki's family treated their guest like a king. Lelani picked lavender orchid blossoms for the table. The family dined on fresh papaya, poi, and a special sweet made by boiling juice from the sugarcane. Akamai liked the sweet. He ate and ate until he grew drowsy.

"Akamai," Moki said, trying to think of a way to save Pekea, "let me give you enough taro from my patch to pay your taxes to the king. My father has more than enough."

"No," Akamai replied. "I cannot take your taro. I am no beggar. I must catch the porpoise."

When the fire died to glowing embers, Akamai fell asleep. Moki thought of hiding Akamai's harpoon, but the stranger slept with his fingers curved around the shaft of the weapon.

The next day Akamai sharpened his harpoon and waited for the hour when Pekea would swim to the coral reef. As the time drew near, another idea flashed into Moki's mind.

"Akamai, you were fond of the sweet we ate last evening," Moki said. "Would you like to help Lelani and me make more of it? You could take it with you to eat on your journey to the king."

Akamai smiled. "I would like that. Let us do it."

Moki asked Lelani to pour the cane syrup into a pot while he built a fire. Moki worked slowly. When the sticky brew bubbled to a boil, he let Akamai help stir it. The stranger stirred for many minutes, then Moki helped him pour the sweet into a giant clam shell to cool.

"It will cool more quickly if we set the clam shell in a pot of cold water," Moki told Akamai.

"I will bring water from the sea," Akamai said. "Time grows short."

While Akamai was away on his errand, Moki and Lelani greased their hands with coconut oil. Then, hiding the oil pot behind a hibiscus bush, they waited. The sweet mass cooled more quickly after Akamai brought the cold water from the sea.

"Now," said Moki at last. "The sweet is cool. We must roll it into small balls." Moki and Lelani dipped their fingers into the clam shell, scooped up mounds of the sweet, and shaped them into balls. Akamai followed their example, but soon he was shouting.

"Ho! What is this! Help!" Akamai danced up and down in surprise and anger. "Why does the sweet stick to my hands and fingers?"

"How unfortunate you are," Moki said. "It does not stick to my fingers, nor to Lelani's." Moki took care to stand in front of the hibiscus bush that hid the pot of coconut oil. "Perhaps the island spirits do not approve of your plans for Pekea the Porpoise."

Akamai rushed to the sea to wash his hands. But the salt water only hardened the mass on his fingers. Moki helped Akamai clean his hands, but he worked slowly. The job was completed only after Pekea the Porpoise had come and gone from the coral reef for the day. As the sun rose high in the sky, Akamai started on his way. He accepted some taro from Moki and hurried forth on his journey to the king.

As soon as the stranger was gone, Moki

splashed into the sea and called to Pekea. After a while his pet appeared and they played in the surf as they had done for many moons."

When Naniloa finished her story she smiled and took a big sip of tea. "You like tale?"

"It was great," Jess replied. "Different from any that I've read in the library books."

With no urging, Naniloa began another story; and when she finished it she started still another. By the time she finished speaking, Jess's notebook was almost full, and Johnny was beginning to squirm in his chair.

"Thank you, Naniloa," Jess said. "You've been a great help to me. How can I ever thank you?"

"It would please me if you would listen to Johnny and me sing. It is not often that I have a fine man to join me in the old songs." Naniloa set her basket aside and picked up a ukulele from a corner of the room. "Will you sing, Johnny? The Hawaiian Wedding Song?"

Johnny nodded, and as Jess listened in amazement, he and Naniloa blended their voices into one of the classic art songs of the islands. Naniloa's soprano soared loud and clear, and Johnny sang the baritone part as if he were a trained musician. Although Jess couldn't understand the Hawaiian words, the beauty of the music brought tears to her eyes.

"We Hawaiians have always loved to sing." Naniloa pulled herself up to her full towering height. "But we seldom get a chance any more. We should sing together more often, Johnny."

"You're right," he agreed. "We should." But Johnny was through singing for the time being, and as he thanked Naniloa for her hospitality at the same time he subtly guided Jess back toward the jeep.

They drove down the valley path in comfortable silence until Jess spoke.

"You never told me you sang, Johnny. You have a beautiful voice. You could be a professional musician."

"I have a degree in music." Johnny shrugged. "Journalism speaks from the mind, but music speaks from the heart. I will use both when the time is right, when the old Hawaii replaces this rat race going on in the islands today. But for the present I just sing to the tourist wahines at the Surfside. They like."

Jess was speechless. She sensed that she

would never really know Johnny Kuhio.

"Do you have to get back home in a hurry?" Johnny broke into Jess's thoughts.

"No, but don't you have to report for work?"

"Not today." Johnny grinned. "I asked for time off. How about driving to Makapuu Point? It's not far from Waikiki. If you plan to use that tale about the porpoise, you should at least know what one looks like. I can show you some at Sea Life Park. You'll be surprised at how smart they are."

"Sounds like fun."

"Do you plan to use the porpoise tale?" Johnny asked.

"I haven't decided yet," Jess said.

"If you do, I'd like to read your final draft of it."

They rode in silence once more until Johnny drove through the entryway to the marine exhibit and found a parking spot.

"This place draws a real crowd." Jess glanced around at the throng of people. "What shall we see first?"

Johnny bought admission tickets, then he guided Jess by the elbow. "Let's take a look at the reef exhibit. It's a duplication of Oahu's coast and offshore reefs. By walking down these steps and ramps we can see three fathoms beneath the ocean's surface and observe octopus and sharks eyeball to eyeball."

Jess followed Johnny, sometimes slowing him down so she could examine a lava flow or some living coral a moment longer. She watched eels swimming near blazing yellow tang fish while limestone caves and coral formations shimmered in the background.

"Fantastic," Jess said. "Utterly fantastic."

"Wait until you see the Ocean Science Theatre." Johnny led Jess to the next attraction where scuba-equipped marine scientists put porpoises through drills using electronic sound signals in preparation for open-ocean research assignments.

"I had no idea porpoises were so intelligent," Jess said as she watched one respond to a learned command. "I'm beginning to believe that Naniloa's porpoise story could have been a true tale."

"I've saved the best for last," Johnny said. "Whaler's Cove."

They threaded their way through the crowd to the cove where blue-green water slapped against the bulwarks of the *Essex*, a replica of a nineteenth century whaling ship. As Jess watched, a huge whale leaped high out of the water to catch a tidbit of fish tossed by a boy sitting high in the ship's rigging.

"Isn't that dangerous?" Jess asked. "There are people swimming in the same water with that whale!"

"They take care," Johnny assured her. "And the whale is tame. But now watch the porpoises." He pointed to their right, where a pretty dark-haired girl dived into the water. Soon four sleek bodies appeared near her. One by one they leaped, somersaulting through the air with graceful spinning movements. Johnny and Jess watched until Jess's feet were numb to the knees.

"I hate to leave, Johnny, but I'm exhausted. Could we sit down for a while?"

Johnny found a lunch counter, where they rested and ordered sandwiches. But the counter was crowded, and as soon as they ate they walked back to the jeep and headed for home.

"It was a wonderful day, Johnny," Jess said as Johnny stopped the jeep in the Wong driveway. "Would you like to come in for a while?"

"I would, but I'm sure I would be unwelcome. Your father and I share a business arrangement, not a friendship."

"I'm sure Dad would accept any friend I brought home," Jess insisted.

"Not this time, Jess. This has been a day I'll remember forever. Let's not spoil it." Johnny leaned to kiss her, and Jess returned the kiss willingly — eagerly.

Once back in her room, Jess kicked off her shoes. Was she falling in love with Johnny? She certainly didn't want to. She wasn't ready to fall in love with any man just yet. She had many things to do before she settled down to married life. She thought of the call she must make to Mr. Higgins and of the resignation letter she must finish and deliver to Reeta. But those things could wait a little longer. Right now she had to transcribe her notebook of folktales before her shorthand went stale and she lost some of the feeling Naniloa had put in her words.

Chapter Thirteen

Jess spent the rest of the weekend reading, transcribing, and revising Hawaiian folktales. Now and then when she opened her desk drawer she would notice her letter from Mr. Higgins and beneath it the rough draft of her resignation, but somehow she couldn't bring herself to type a final copy of the resignation letter.

On Monday morning Jess was not surprised when Alex treated her coolly, speaking to her only when absolutely necessary. But after their coffee break he stopped at her desk.

"Jess, I'm going to drive to a plantation to get info on one of the pineapple planters. I'd like you to come along and take notes. The more you know about the industry, the more valuable you'll be to Pine Pack."

"Okay, Alex." Jess drew a line on her memo calendar marking the last chore she had completed, then she walked with Alex to the company car.

"Is the plantation far from here?" she asked as he drove into the traffic.

"It's nearby in the valley," Alex said. "It's one of the oldest plantations in the islands. Dates back to the late 1800s. Bob Storewell owns it, and he's the one I'll interview."

"How many canneries are there in the islands?" Jess asked.

"Six major ones. Eight plantations keep them supplied with fruit. The pineapple industry provides employment for nearly twenty-five thousand people, and it's second only to sugar."

"Alex, when you saw me and Johnny last Friday night, we were on business." Jess blurted the words, feeling the need to clear her conscience.

"Did someone dispute that fact?" Alex gazed straight ahead.

"I thought you might," Jess said. "You've been giving me the Arctic chill all morning, and now you're spouting pineapple statistics instead of what's really on your mind."

"Oh! So now you can read my mind?"

"You know what I mean. Johnny took me to the library Friday, then we went to the beach to talk with Naniloa about folktales. She's been a great help to me."

"You needn't explain." Alex shrugged. "I guess you noticed that I wasn't sitting home counting coconuts."

Jess laughed, and the tension between

them eased. "Seriously, Alex, I don't want you to think I was giving you the run-around. I had no intention of going out Friday night until Johnny offered to help me do folktale research."

"Forget it, Jess. I'd like to read some of your stories. How about it? Have you finished any of them yet?"

Jess shook her head. "Not yet, but I'll meet Dad's deadline."

Jess gazed across acres of low, blue-green plants as Alex turned the car onto a winding dirt road that twisted through the pineapple fields. To her right Jess watched men following a truck which pulled a harvesting boom machine. The huge boom arm extended into the field where the men picked the ripe fruit, snapped off the crowns, and placed the pineapple on a conveyor belt. As Jess watched, the fruit traveled along the conveyor until it was eased into the truck bin.

"So this is harvest time?" Jess asked.

"Plantations have many harvest times," Alex replied. "The planters manage their crop so that different fields of fruit ripen at different times. That way the canneries have a constant supply of pineapple. The time between picking and canning is seldom more than three or four hours."

181

As they turned into another field Jess saw a middle-aged man stooped over a row of small plants. "What's he doing?" she asked. "Why is the ground covered with plastic?"

"That's Bob Storewell," Alex said. "I'll let you ask him those questions. While you talk to him, I'll get a picture for the paper."

Alex stopped the car, helped Jess out, then guided her carefully between the plastic strips to where Mr. Storewell was working. After explaining their mission to him, Alex introduced Jess and nodded to her to begin the interview.

"Mr. Storewell, how long have you worked this plantation?" Jess made a note of Mr. Storewell's sun- and wind-seamed face.

"I've worked here for twenty-five years." Mr. Storewell rubbed his back. "But some days it seems like fifty. At least two days a week I work right along with my hired men. Some owners are experimenting with mechanical planters, but so far I can outdo any machine they've come up with. I can put six to eight thousand suckers in the ground during an eight-hour day."

"Wouldn't it be easier to plant seeds?" Jess asked.

"Easier, but about eight years slower," Mr. Storewell replied. "It takes a pineapple plant ten years to mature if grown from seed. That luxury is reserved for beds where experimental plants are being tested and observed. But here in my fields, I push suckers or pineapple slips through holes in this plastic. They produce a mature plant in eighteen months."

"Why the plastic?" Jess asked.

"It helps in controlling weeds. Of course the soil is also fumigated to kill root parasites."

"Do you have a family?" Jess asked, pen poised.

"Yes. My wife teaches at Fragrant Tree School, and we have one married daughter and one son in college on the mainland."

Alex stepped forward and asked Mr. Storewell to pose for him, and as the planter did so, Alex snapped his picture. He took two more shots, then thanked the man.

"Mr. Storewell, do you have any hobbies?" Jess asked.

"I'm a camera bug. I free-lance color slides to travel magazines on the mainland. I'm president of the Honolulu Camera Club this year."

"Thank you very much for your time, Mr. Storewell," Alex said, helping Jess end her interview. "You'll be seeing your picture in the paper soon. Watch for it."

When Jess and Alex were back in the car,

Jess looked at her notes as if she couldn't believe what she had jotted down.

"Surprised?" Alex asked.

"Am I! I was expecting to meet more of a peasant type."

"That's why I brought you along. These pineapple growers work hard, and they pay their fieldhands excellent wages. They maintain a high standard of living and take part in civic activities." Alex looked at his watch. "It's past noon. Shall we stop at a drive-in and grab a sandwich?"

"Fine with me." Jess tried to mentally digest all she had discovered at the pineapple fields as Alex drove toward the city. She was still deep in thought when Alex spoke.

"There's Johnny."

Jess glanced up and saw three beach boys strolling across the white sand of the Surfside's beach area. They looked so much alike in dress, motions, mannerisms that it took Jess several moments to realize which one was Johnny. She waved, but Alex turned a corner and Johnny didn't see her.

"How about a date for tonight?" Alex asked after he had driven back to Pine Pack and parked the car.

"I'd love to go out, Alex, but I'm still working on those folktales. It's a time-consuming project."

"Do it on company hours," Alex insisted.

"I would if I could, but my afternoon schedule is crammed full. There's no time for reading or writing."

"Then how about a late date?" Alex asked. "I could use the early part of the evening for developing these films and printing some pictures. If you'd let me pick you up about nine-thirty, we could have a late dinner at Fisherman's Wharf. How about that?"

"You're a hard man to resist." Jess laughed. "I'd love it."

Reeta gave Jess a dirty look as Jess slipped back into the office and checked her memo pad. Her in basket was filled, and her out basket was empty.

"You've thrown the whole PR office a half-day behind." Reeta brushed a silvery strand of hair from her forehead. "I hope your sashay into the fields was meaningful and enlightening."

"I'll have this work out by five o'clock," Jess said.

"I had hoped you'd have it out before then," Reeta said. "I have three more numbers for you to call about recipes."

Jess felt herself flushing. Why should Reeta's recipes come before her own folktales! "Perhaps you'd rather call the numbers yourself just in case I don't get everything caught up," Jess said. "The big meeting with Dad is day after tomorrow."

"I'm sure you'll find time to make three phone calls between now and then," Reeta said.

Jess controlled her temper and managed to get her own work finished as well as to make Reeta's calls for her. But when the dismissal buzzer sounded, she hurried from the office, ignoring Reeta.

Once at home, Jess asked Ora to bring a snack tray to her room so she could work undisturbed through the dinner hour. Later, when Malia stopped by to say hello, Jess let her read some of the folktales she had completed.

"Well, what do you think?" Jess asked. "Like them?"

"I think they're great." Malia kicked her shoes off. "The problem is going to be deciding on the best one."

"I'll let Dad do that." Jess laughed. She was relieved when Malia left her room and went to her studio to practice. She didn't feel like telling her that she was going out with Alex. And the fact that she was reluctant to mention her date made her feel guilty. This would be no business meeting. She was falling more and more under Alex's

186

spell, and she was beginning to sense that his interest in her had nothing to do with public relations or Pine Pack.

Jess heard Alex's car ease into the driveway promptly at nine-thirty, and she raised her long skirt and hurried outside before he had a chance to come to the door.

"I'd like to think you're eager to see me," Alex said, "but I suspect that you only hurried out because you're starved."

"Perhaps a bit of both." Jess slipped into the car, hoping that Malia was still in her studio. "I hope Fisherman's Wharf specializes in seafood."

"Right." Alex headed the car toward the Kewalo Basin and they soon reached the restaurant. Alex asked for a table that overlooked the ocean, and the manager led them to an ideal spot. After they ordered, Jess sat peering across the water, then she looked around inside the restaurant.

"This place is absolutely fascinating, Alex. Look on the walls. Harpoons. Nets. Buoys."

"The owners have collected all those things over a period of years," Alex said. "If they ever get tired of cooking they can open a museum."

Jess couldn't remember enjoying a dinner as much as she did this one, and she suspected that her enjoyment was due as much to Alex's company as to the excellent lobster. She lingered over every morsel of her dinner, and the restaurant was about to close by the time she and Alex finished their dessert and their last sips of coffee.

Once they were back in the car Alex drove slowly into the hills until he came to a promontory that overlooked the sea. He stopped the car, and they sat in the beauty of the moon-drenched night for several moments without speaking.

"Jess," Alex said, at last breaking the silence. "I have something for you."

Jess turned toward Alex. His tone of voice told her that he was about to say something important. "What is it?"

Alex reached into his jacket pocket and pulled out a chain with a ring dangling from it. "It's a friendship ring. As you know, I've dated a lot of girls, but I've never felt that I wanted to make any lasting commitment until I met you."

"Stop, Alex." Jess struggled for the right words. "Before you say more, let me tell you that I have no intention of marrying. At least not in the near future."

"I've already guessed that. But neither am I ready for marriage. This is just a friendship ring. Would you consider going steady with me? I'm not promising marriage or demanding any promises from you. I'd just like to see you exclusively in the future. Will you consider it?"

"I don't know what to say," Jess said. "You know I'm fond of you."

"Fondness could grow into love," Alex said.

Jess held the ring on the palm of her hand studying it, a jade heart in a silver setting. Was she ready to narrow her field to only one man? She thought of Malia and of Johnny.

But what about Johnny? She liked him. She couldn't deny that. But all her reasons for liking him were superficial — his looks, his velvet-soft voice, his prowess in the surf. When Jess faced the facts, she knew in her heart that Johnny was chasing an impossible, unrealistic dream. Nobody could walk forward into the past as Johnny was trying to do.

At first Jess had thought Johnny was unique, but now she knew even that wasn't true. He was so like the other members of his peer group that she had had trouble picking him out of a group of three. But the fact that bothered Jess most was that Johnny at age thirty was still content to be in school. Although she hated to admit it, she knew that Johnny could only function as a beach boy or as a scholar in the halls of ivy. In the corridors of life, he would be unable to relate to reality.

"Jess?"

"Yes?"

"I'd like to know what's going on in that head of yours. You've been quiet for so long."

"I've been thinking." Jess smiled up at him. "Thinking that I'd love to wear your jade ring around my neck." She leaned toward Alex, and he opened his arms to her.

Chapter Fourteen

It was late when Jess fell asleep that night, and the next morning she could hardly drag herself from bed. She ate Ora's breakfast with only one eye open, but when she sat beside her father on the ride to the cannery she came to full attention.

"I'd like to have a preview of your folktales, Jess. Do you have any of them ready?"

"They're all almost ready. I'm going to retype them for the meeting, but you're welcome to see the rough copies any time."

"You haven't been leaving them at the office overnight, have you?"

Jess patted her straw purse. "Indeed not. I have them right here. Want me to read them to you?"

"Not enough time. We're almost at the cannery. But, I'm flying to Maui today to visit some independent growers who supply us with fruit. I want you to make the flight with me. That way we'll be insured of privacy. I have a feeling that things are about to explode in the PR department. You haven't let anyone read your stories, have you?"

"Only Malia." Jess couldn't bear to tell her dad that both Johnny and Alex had asked to read the tales. "Of course, Johnny helped me find books and he heard the tales Naniloa told, but he hasn't read my adaptations."

"Good," Mr. Wong said. "Don't let them out of your sight. Copying your stories would be much easier than doing all the research necessary to gather the tales from scratch. I don't want anyone else to profit from your labor. And I don't want Pine Pack to be scooped, to be put in the position of searching again for the big new idea."

"When is the flight to Maui?" Jess asked.

"About mid-morning." Mr. Wong glanced at his watch. "Do your mail routings, then come to my office. Maui is about seventy miles from here. The flight will take only a few minutes."

Jess's fingers shook as she opened the mail, but Reeta didn't seem to notice.

"Did you get your stories finished?" Reeta asked.

"Almost," Jess said. "I just have to do the final typing."

"Why not let me do that for you?" Reeta offered. "You've helped me so much on the recipes. I'd be happy to reciprocate."

Jess kept her voice even. "That won't be

necessary, Reeta. I'll manage." Jess hoped Reeta couldn't hear her heart pounding. She had hated it when Johnny and Alex had asked to see the stories, but now that Reeta had made a try, she felt better. There was no more suspicion on one person than on another.

"Ready, Jess?" Her father stood in the doorway, shifting his weight from one foot to the other.

"Didn't mean to keep you waiting, Dad." Jess stood, picked up her purse and started to leave the office. "Dad and I'll be away for a few hours, Reeta. I'll tend to my in basket when I return."

"We're going to Maui, Reeta," Mr. Wong said. "Routine trip."

Jess hurried from the office. She loved to go to the airport just to watch the throngs of people. Today, slit-skirted Chinese women were alighting from a plane, and ahead of them a Japanese family carrying straw suitcases was met by island relatives. Jess smelled the mingled perfume of ginger, jasmine, and plumeria, and she was so engrossed in the scene at hand that she laughed in pleasure and surprise when her father slipped an orchid lei around her neck.

Aboard the plane Jess felt the floorboards vibrate as the props spun and the engines roared. The smell of diesel exhaust wafted into the plane, but it disappeared once they were airborne.

"Dad!" Jess cried suddenly. "There's an island beneath us. Maui already?"

Her father leaned forward to look. "No. That's Lanai. It's owned by the Dole Corporation. They've done great things there — transformed a semi-wasteland into a huge pineapple plantation."

Lanai was barely out of sight when the jewel that was Maui appeared before Jess's eyes. The plane banked for landing, touched down gently, and braked to a smooth stop.

"I'm going to rent a car and show you the island," her dad said. "I'll hire a driver-guide, and while you sightsee, I'll read those stories with no worry about being spied upon."

Once her dad had engaged a car and driver, Jess sat in the back seat with her dad while the driver sat alone in front.

"Jess, this is Henry Lung, our driver."

"I'm pleased to meet you, Henry," Jess replied.

"Take us on any basic tour, Henry," Mr. Wong said. "We have business to transact, but interrupt whenever there's an interesting scene. Jess is a newcomer to the island."

Jess pulled the folktales from her purse, and while her dad was engrossed in reading them, she gazed at the passing scene.

"Ahead of us is Haleakala," Henry said. "It is a volcano, but no worry. Last erupted in sixteen hundreds."

"How deep is the crater?" Jess asked.

"Three thousand feet deep. Twenty miles from rim to rim. We are gaining altitude. Now look behind you."

Jess looked back and down on fields of taro plants, their green leaves shimmering in the sun. Then as they drove on she admired lush vegetation and groves of guava trees.

"Stop at Lahaina," Mr. Wong said, looking from his reading.

Henry drove a few miles farther, then parked the car at a small coastal town wedged between cane and pineapple fields. "This spot a favorite of King Kamehameha I. He established headquarters here at Lahaina. The capital wasn't moved to Honolulu until 1845."

When Henry stopped speaking, Mr. Wong and Jess left the car and strolled toward a quay where fishing boats and yachts were anchored in a snug harbor. As they sat down on a bench, Mr. Wong spoke.

"I like all of these stories, Jess. My guess is

that they'll be far more popular than the recipes."

"Anyone could steal these tales, Dad. They're in public domain."

"We can't copyright them before they're published," Mr. Wong said. "I checked the law about that."

Jess stared across the watery roads where whales used to play. She felt a certain loyalty to Johnny. They were still friends. She fingered Alex's ring and felt even a greater loyalty to him. But as long as she was on the Pine Pack payroll she knew she must do her best for the company.

"I have a thought, Dad. I hate the idea of trapping anyone, but it appears that it's going to be necessary. Why don't you begin publication of the folktale booklets. Begin today. After all, you like the stories. Whoever our traitor is, he'll be expecting no action until after tomorrow's meeting."

"That doesn't give us much of a head start," her father said.

"But every minute would count. And I have another idea. At tomorrow's meeting I'll read a folktale that's not of this group. I found some that are still under copyright. I'm guessing that our informer secretly will be taping whatever I read. You could pretend to okay the story. If all is well, no harm

196

will be done. But if someone is trying to scoop us, my guess is that they'll rush their tape to whoever it is who is hiring them as soon as the meeting ends."

"But Commercial Can will still come up with folktale booklets," her dad said. "We'll be left out."

Jess shook her head. "Commercial Can will have published stolen material. You can tip off the original publisher. Of course Commercial Can could dodge their troubles by paying a fee to the original publisher, but there would be a time-consuming legal tangle, and there would also be a lot of negative publicity."

"A legal battle would take time," Mr. Wong admitted. "During that time we could publish your story adaptations; and at the same time we might be able to find out who's responsible for the leak."

Jess's heart felt like a ball of lead. She was glad her dad liked her ideas, but what if Alex was the person they caught? Mentally Jess began planning the final wording of her resignation letter. The only thing for her to do was to leave Pine Pack. She should have turned her letter in before this.

"I have one more idea, Jess. At the meeting I want you to read only a short synopsis of the tale you plan to present. It's my guess that the guilty person will ask to hear the entire story. If that happens it would make our search easier."

"Okay, Dad. That's the way I'll do it."

Jess and her dad ate a light lunch in Lahaina, then Mr. Wong transacted his business. It was past mid-afternoon when Henry drove them back to the airport, and when they reached Honolulu, Mr. Wong drove Jess home instead of to the office.

"Use my office, Jess. When you're through typing the stories lock them in my desk drawer."

"Right, Dad." Jess went inside while her father drove on to Pine Pack. Once she was seated at her father's desk, her fingers shook on the typewriter keys. What was she doing? Whom did she expect to catch in this trap she was building?

Chapter Fifteen

Jess dreaded facing the next day at the office, yet there would be relief in having the meeting over, of having the tension end. She had completed her letter of resignation and at the first unobtrusive moment she planned to drop it into Reeta's in basket. That decision alone should have relieved her mind, but somehow it didn't.

Jess expected that the PR meeting would be scheduled for the first thing in the morning, but when she reached her desk she found a memo stating that her father would meet with PR personnel following the afternoon coffee break.

Just as Jess was wondering how she could exist until three P.M., Reeta hurried to her desk, heels clicking and blonde hair flowing.

"The galleys for the company brochure are ready to be corrected. Do you have time to work on them this morning?"

Jess checked her day's schedule. "At ten o'clock I have an interview with the safety director, and at eleven-thirty I'm to cover a university luncheon where our assistant personnel director is speaking."

"You can begin proofing the galleys as soon as you've sorted the mail. Do as much as you can, then fit the rest of it into your day as you would any continuing assignment."

Jess nodded, glad for plenty of work to occupy her until the afternoon PR meeting. The galleys were in good order; she found few errors in the pages she had time to read.

Later in the morning Jess's interview with the safety director went smoothly. Mr. Akimo was a vital, interesting man, and Jess met him armed with pertinent questions concerning safety equipment, new innovations in plant facilities that had been designed to protect the workers, statistics on injuries, and safety awards.

The morning passed like a slow-moving cargo ship. At the university luncheon, Jess found herself taking notes on the personnel director's speech in a very personal way. The director's subject was *Do You Measure Up?* and Jess asked herself the same questions she felt the students must be asking themselves.

Initiative? Jess hoped she had that. She was quite willing to take the first step in a new project, but she realized that sometimes she hesitated to start things without being told to do so.

Persistence? The personnel director spoke glibly, but Jess became lost in her own thoughts on the subject. An enduring continuance was certainly not to be confused with a stubborn refusal to yield.

As the speech continued, Jess smiled to herself. Everyone thought that he had drive and ambition. And who would admit to being an unobjective thinker, who would admit that his attitude was inflexible?

"You must have an interest in service," the personnel director continued, grabbing Jess's attention once again. "Most PR activities involve others; you as an individual are secondary to your publics. Your friendliness, your ability to do a variety of tasks, and your lack of self-consciousness all prove your interest in service."

The personnel director concluded her speech with a quotation from Aldous Huxley, and Jess's pen flew across the page to copy it down. "Every man who knows how to read has it in his power to magnify himself, to multiply the ways in which he exists, to make his life full, significant and interesting."

Jess slipped away from the meeting asking herself how she measured up. She had been in PR for several months. She had written a letter of resignation, but she had not presented it to her superior. Perhaps she should change her mind. How did she measure up? Would she be more successful in teaching than in PR work? She was still thinking about the question when her father entered the office and called to order the meeting they had all been anticipating.

"You all know what happened to Reeta's idea of sponsoring a series of concerts," Mr. Wong began. "I'm hoping that the rest of our ideas will come to a more successful conclusion. Alex, we'll start with you. Can you show us a mock-up of one of the news ads you had in mind?"

"Yes, sir. I have one right here." Alex unfolded a large paper that held a full-length glossy print of the planter he and Jess had interviewed in the pineapple fields. Much white space framed the picture, and a brief paragraph of biographical information on Mr. Storewell stood out in bold type.

"I like it, Alex," Mr. Wong said. "You've used a unique approach. Its simplicity is eyecatching. Call a messenger and send it to the paper immediately. Ask that it appear as soon as possible. Then get to work on similar layouts that will include both plantation owners and fieldhands."

Jess smiled at Alex. Although she had

helped with his interview, he had given her no clue as to how his finished layout would look. She admired his ability to keep a secret.

"Reeta, how is the recipe pamphlet coming along?" Mr. Wong looked expectantly at Reeta.

"It couldn't be better," Reeta replied. "I've collected recipes from many of the socially prominent families in Honolulu. It required hours of telephoning, but I think the results are worth all the work I put into the project."

Jess tried to squelch her irritation as Reeta claimed full credit for all the work on the recipe project.

"I've received recipes for pineapple upside-down cake, pineapple pie, pineapple crunch. There's even a main-course recipe featuring pineapple and rice, and of course there are many pineapple-based salad recipes. I think housewives will appreciate this collection."

"It sounds fine, Reeta," Mr. Wong agreed. "I'd like to have a copy of the recipes. I'll have my housekeeper test each one for accuracy."

"But that'll take forever." Reeta's voice trembled. "Don't you trust these ladies who were so good as to contribute the recipes?"

"Of course I trust them," Mr. Wong said. "But anyone can make a mistake. I'll ask Ora to test the recipes. It won't take her long. She loves to cook. I may have part of the results brought here to the cannery so we all can sample the finished products."

"That sounds like a good idea to me." Alex nodded.

"Jess." Mr. Wong spoke, and everyone looked at Jess. "What luck did you have with your folktale idea?"

"I found some tales that I consider appropriate and appealing to children." Jess tapped the sheaf of papers in her hand. "These are lengthy. Let me give you a brief synopsis of some of the plots. In *Feast for Iolani*, a great fuss is being made over who will sit at the head of the table when Iolani's subjects come for a gala meal. With the help of the High Kahuna, Iolani solves the problem with wisdom and diplomacy. Another tale is called *The City of Refuge*. It tells how two refugees cleverly escape their pursuers and reach the haven of the City of Refuge."

"You really are telling us nothing," Reeta complained. "I want to hear at least one story in its entirety. That's the only way to be sure whether or not it's appropriate."

Jess's heart leaped, and at the same

moment she felt guilty. She hated to trap anyone, yet if it had to be one of her co-workers . . . Johnny interrupted her thoughts.

"I think the summary is good enough. Jess would know what would appeal to kids. After all she's a trained teacher."

"No," Alex protested. "Reeta's right. I think we all should take time to hear at least one story from beginning to end."

Jess's mouth was so dry she could hardly speak. Surely Johnny had eliminated himself from suspicion. Reeta? Alex? She couldn't bear it if Alex were the one.

"Choose one tale and read the whole thing, Jess," her father said.

Jess nodded and began.

The Pearl of Great Beauty

Long ago on the Hawaiian island of Kauai there lived an old, old woman and her grandson, Keroko. Keroko loved his island home, but he longed to see the world. One day he told his grandmother of his dream.

"Grandmother, I must leave Kauai. I must seek my fortune in the land across the sea."

Grandmother shook her head. "You

know nothing of the outer world. The sea can be both friend and foe. Do not go."

"I have built a koa-wood canoe," Keroko replied. "It is light. It is sturdy. It will carry me to distant lands."

"You do not know the way," Grandmother said. "You will become lost and perish in the sea."

"Mano, the shark spirit, will guide me." With a stick Keroko drew a picture of a shark in the sand. "Mano will keep me safe. Tomorrow when the Great Star of Kane rises in the east, I will go."

Grandmother sighed and laid her hand on his shoulder. "I see that you are determined. You have my blessing. Perhaps it is best for you to go. But first, I have a gift for you."

These words surprised Keroko, for he and his grandmother were very poor. "What sort of a gift, Grandmother?"

"It is a pearl of great beauty," his grandmother said. "You must go to the Lagoon of Kanaloa and there seek the entrance to a hidden cave. Inside the cave on a high, rock-strewn ledge you will see a conch shell. Inside the shell, wrapped in a pandanus leaf you will find the pearl of great beauty. Bring it to me that I may see it once again, then it is yours."

Keroko did not believe his grandmother. But he was an obedient boy and the Lagoon of Kanaloa was nearby. Keroko reached it as the tide was going out. Wading into the blue waters of the palm-fringed lagoon, he swam to a spot where a sheer cliff thrust toward the sky. But search as he might, he found no cave.

His grandmother was getting old. The pearl and the cave must have been only a dream. The cool water felt like satin against Keroko's warm skin. He floated on his back, thinking about the adventure that awaited him at sunrise.

As the shadows of afternoon fell across the lagoon, the tide was at lowest ebb. Tiny white crabs scampered sideways across the honey-colored sand, and seashells glistened in the sunlight. Keroko was about to pull himself from the water when he spied a half-moon opening in the side of the cliff. Could this be Grandmother's hidden cave? With clean, hard strokes Keroko swam to the opening and eased his body through it.

As his eyes adjusted to the dimness, Keroko saw that he was in an arched chamber eerie with soft blue light. Water sounds echoed from wall to wall. It was a moment before he spied the pink conch shell perched high on a rocky ledge.

Keroko scrambled up the lava rock, picked up the shell and removed a round object wrapped in a crumbling pandanus leaf. His fingers shook as he unwrapped the pearl. Grandmother had told the truth. The pearl gave off a luminous glow as Keroko rolled it in the palm of his hand.

Keroko stared at the pearl for several moments before he noticed that the cave was growing dark. The half-moon opening he had slipped through was almost closed by the incoming tide. Popping the pearl into his mouth, Keroko dived into the water. Fighting his way through the cave entrance, he surfaced in the still lagoon.

Keroko hastened back to the thatched hut where his grandmother waited. His heart pounded like a temple drum.

"Grandmother!" Keroko shouted as he ran into the hut. "I found it. I found your pearl of great beauty."

Grandmother held out her wrinkled brown hand to receive the gem, and together they admired it. Its milky luster seemed to change from pink to blue to green and back to luminous white.

"How long have you known about this

pearl?" Keroko asked.

"Since I was a young girl." Grand-mother placed the pearl in the center of the table. "My grandmother gave it to me."

"But why have you not sold it?" Keroko asked. "It is a gem fit for a king. It would have brought you great wealth."

"I have never been poor," Grand-mother replied. "Whenever trouble came to me, I would think of my pearl. The thought of such great beauty gave me strength. I knew I could sell this gem. But somehow my need was never that great. The pearl was like a rainbow in my mind."

Keroko held the pearl between his thumb and forefinger and admired it. Surely it would bring a great price.

"Now the pearl is yours." Grand-mother's gentle voice broke into his thoughts. "I have made a pouch for you to carry it in. You must put this pearl to more practical use than I did." She dropped the pearl into the pouch. "You must find the village of Lahaina on an island called Maui. There you must sell the pearl to the captain of a whaling ship."

Keroko thanked his grandmother. That night he slept with the pearl of great beauty under his pillow of palm fronds. Dreams of wealth and riches filled his sleep, but when he awakened he felt a strange sweet sadness.

As the Great Star of Kane rose in the east, Grandmother gave Keroko some food wrapped in fresh leaves. Keroko thanked her, then bade her farewell. After carefully tying the pearl of great beauty in the pouch at his waist, he dragged his koa-wood canoe into the water. With one last look at his grandmother and his home, he paddled beyond the breakers into the green waters.

Far out at sea Keroko paused for several moments deep in thought. Then, turning the canoe, he headed for the Lagoon of Kanaloa. At low tide he swam into the hidden cave. Wrapping the pearl of great beauty in a fresh leaf that he had brought with him, he hid it inside the conch shell. He knew he could never bear to sell the pearl. Perhaps one day he would give it to his own son.

It was long past mid-day when Keroko again paddled beyond the breakers to the deep water. He pointed his canoe toward the distant horizon where sky and water met.

That night the moon touched the sea

swells with a luminous glow. Keroko's heart was full. A new world of adventure lay before him. But as he peered into the future, he knew that the beauty he saw came from a rainbow in his mind.

When Jess stopped reading everyone was silent for a few moments, then Reeta spoke.

"It'll never do, Jess. Never. The basic concept is much beyond children. The story would leave them with nothing."

"I disagree," Alex said. "The concept is a mature one, but I think children as well as adults will be impressed with it."

"I agree," Mr. Wong said. "You've done a good job, Jess. I think I'll publish this one story as sort of a pilot pamphlet. We'll see how it goes. The consumers will be the ultimate judges of its success."

The meeting broke up just as the dismissal buzzer sounded. Jess got her purse. In the general confusion of leaving the office, she hoped nobody noticed as she dropped a sealed envelope into Reeta's in basket. She had made her decision. Public relations was not for her. Her resignation would be in official hands in the morning.

Chapter Sixteen

"Jess!" Alex looked at her questioningly as he caught up with her at the front door of the office. "I called to you three times."

"Sorry, Alex! Guess I didn't hear you. That meeting left me uptight."

"Your story was great. I wish we had taken time to hear the others you had adapted. But how about celebrating your success? Let's go on a picnic. I'll order a box lunch from the Surfside, then I'll pick you up in about an hour. How about it?"

Jess wanted nothing more than to spend a quiet evening at home, but some of Alex's enthusiasm rubbed off on her. "Okay, Alex. I'll be ready. I'll ride on home with Dad."

On the drive home Mr. Wong grinned at Jess. "I think we pulled that off rather well. What do you think?"

"I suppose we did. I hated to have to do it."

"And I hated to have to ask you to, but I can't afford to have someone undermine one of the most important aspects of my business."

"How soon do you think we'll know who . . ." Jess hesitated. "But maybe we're wrong, Dad. Maybe no one's after any of the ideas presented today."

"I hope you're right," her dad replied. "We should know soon. Within a day or two. Someone may be on their way to the printer right now."

At the house Jess visited with Malia for a few moments, then she took a relaxing tub bath and dressed in a fresh slacks outfit before Alex arrived. She hadn't told Malia about Alex's friendship ring, but she knew she would have to do so soon.

"Where to?" Jess asked as she climbed into Alex's car.

"Thought we'd try Maile Beach," Alex said. "It's in a small valley on the north shore. The area is less crowded than some. Smell those roast-beef sandwiches? I'm starving."

Jess inhaled the mouth-watering aroma and tried to forget the PR office and all its tensions. They drove to the beach and parked the car just off the road above the soft sand.

"Looks as if someone saved this place just for us." Jess picked up the box lunch and thermos bottle and followed Alex through the sand toward the sea.

Alex spread a blanket underneath a palm tree, turned on his radio, and helped Jess unpack the lunch. "If I were a musician I would have brought my guitar and we would sing in the twilight."

"At this point I'd just as soon eat." Jess laughed and bit into one of the sandwiches. She ate slowly, savoring the flavor of each morsel.

When they had finished eating, Alex stretched out on the blanket and closed his eyes while Jess gazed at the vast expanse of ocean and listened to the soft music pouring from the radio. Alex was quiet for so long that Jess knew he must be asleep. After a while she rose and walked toward the wet-packed sand. She had never seen the ocean look like this before. She started to go back to waken Alex, then she thought better of it. He was tired, and he would only laugh and remind her that the tide came in and the tide went out. It was to be expected.

But all the same Jess watched the water with interest. It looked as if someone had pulled the plug from the ocean floor. The waves seemed to be draining away, leaving the shore. Jess wondered at the reef, which was emptier than she had ever seen it before. But when she saw a large fish trapped in a small puddle, she could contain her curiosity no longer.

"Alex!" She ran back to their blanket and shook Alex gently by the shoulder. "Alex! Wake up. There's a big fish trapped down on the shore. I think maybe it's a shark. Come look!"

Alex rubbed his eyes and smiled up at Jess. But when he stood and studied the shoreline, he gasped in horror and grabbed her by the wrist.

"Run, Jess. Come on! Run for your life! We're getting a big one." Alex dashed across the sand, dragging Jess along with him.

Jess's lungs felt as if they were going to burst when at last they reached the car. Alex revved the motor and took off with a spinning of tires.

"Alex! What is it? What's the matter? The blanket — your radio . . ."

"Tidal wave," Alex said, his voice barely a whisper. "It's going to be a big one. The sea is sucking the water from the shoreline to feed a monstrous wave."

"Where are we going?" Jess asked. "How bad will it be?"

"We're going to the radio station. Maybe they can broadcast a warning before the wave hits, but I doubt it. People in the valleys will be trapped."

Alex sped through traffic, unmindful of rules of courtesy. Abandoning his car in front of the radio station, he pulled Jess with him as he dashed into the office.

"Tidal wave!" he shouted. "Put out a warning!"

"Warnings are out, buddy," a radio man replied. "Where have you been? The wave's already hit some spots."

"Then broadcast a notice to Pine Pack workers," Alex shouted. "Tell them they may take refuge in the cannery. Get it on the air, will you?" Alex pulled Pine Pack credentials from his pocket and flashed them at the man.

"Yes, sir."

Alex hardly heard the reply. Again pulling Jess along, he dashed for his car. By this time traffic was hopelessly snarled. Pure luck and a thorough knowledge of the city enabled him to find the alleys and byways to take them to high ground.

"Are we going to the cannery?" Jess asked.

"If it's still there, we'll go to it."

"But it's a long way from the beach," Jess said. "Surely . . ."

For a moment Alex slowed the car and they watched the wave engulf the land from the safety of a hillside promontory.

"Look at it come!" Alex pounded the steering wheel in frustration. "It isn't a towering wave like ones you've read about or seen in movies, but you can't imagine the force behind it."

In the brief moments that they watched, Jess saw the water fill the reef. And it kept coming, submerging the sand, the roads, the fields.

"In low areas and valleys it'll swamp complete villages," Alex said. "Where the water can spread out, the destruction will be less than where it's confined — in the valleys. Let's get to Pine Pack if we can."

Alex drove as far as he dared, then he left the car on a high hill and they began walking. As they neared the water, they tried to keep dry, but it was impossible. The sea poured in relentlessly. Jess felt it swirl about her ankles, her knees, her thighs. Debris floated crazily inland, rattan chairs, bamboo tables, a child's rocking horse. When the water reached her waist, Jess began to panic.

"It'll get worse before it gets better," Alex promised. "But look!" He pointed to the distance. "I can still see part of Pine Pack. The offices may be submerged, but the buildings terraced into the hillside are still above water. We'd better grab hold of something. Grab hold and hang on."

Jess wrapped her arms and legs around a palm tree and felt the water surge around her shoulders.

"Alex!" Jess screamed as the stench of the sea filled her nostrils and dirty brine splashed into her mouth. "Alex! Where are you?"

"I'm okay." Alex shouted from a few feet away where he was clinging to another tree. "Let the water buoy you up. Get a higher hold on the tree, but hang on tight. When this wave leaves, the water will suck back to the shore with tremendous force. Hang on."

The next moments were worse than any nightmare Jess had ever dreamed. As Alex had promised, the wave began to suck back. It tugged at her body, tore at her arms and legs, then threatened to force her to loosen her grip. But she hung on. A scream rose in her throat as a car came floating toward her. Surely she would be crushed between it and the tree. But at the last moment it veered, missing her by inches.

Then the water began to recede. She was safe. Alex was safe. As soon as they could slog through the water they headed on toward Pine Pack. When Alex tried to run, Jess tried to keep up. She slipped frequently and fell, but each time Alex pulled her to her feet and they forged ahead.

When at last they reached the cannery, they paused in terror and dismay. In the front offices windows had been smashed and the sea had flooded in through the rooms and back out again.

"How horrible!" For the first time Jess felt tears welling in her eyes, and her throat constricted until she couldn't speak.

"But the offices were vacated," Alex pointed out. "And the cannery hasn't been touched. Let's get to work."

"Doing what?" Jess asked.

"Clearing as much floor area as we can," Alex replied. "Before long the homeless will begin pouring in here. We'll want to give refuge to as many families as possible."

While Jess and Alex were moving bins of pineapple, cartons of cans, and other portable equipment, Mr. Wong and Malia dashed in.

"Jess! Alex!" Mr. Wong shouted. "Thank heaven you're safe."

There was no time for talking. People were beginning to pour in. Men swore, women wept, and children screamed, their eyes wide with terror. Jess saw the Puno family, the Kapalana brothers. These were people she knew. But they hadn't come just for refuge. They had come to help Pine Pack. Kelli Puno organized the homeless into small groups. The Kapalana twins sought out the injured and brought them to the nurse's office.

Malia opened the first-aid quarters, and she and Jess tried to supply makeshift bandages for the injured, to treat minor wounds and abrasions. The seriously injured, they helped to a more secluded area. While they did these duties, Alex and Mr. Wong tried to organize the throng of people into a semblance of order.

Suddenly Johnny appeared, his long hair dripping water and seaweed. He stared at them with glazed eyes. "My stringbook!" he cried. "It's in the front office. My clippings! I've got to save them." Johnny dashed toward the front office, leaving Jess and Malia stunned.

"He's flipped," Malia said. "Who could worry about clippings and a scrapbook at a time like this?"

"Johnny could," Jess whispered. "Johnny would naturally worry about his education."

After the panic began to subside Ora brought in coffee, and Jess helped distribute it. Just when she thought she couldn't move another muscle, Johnny dashed back to the nurse's quarters.

"Reeta's hurt!" he shouted. "She's in the PR office. I think she must have been there when the water came. I think she's . . . dead."

Chapter Seventeen

Jess stared at Johnny in disbelief. Reeta in the PR room? How could she have been? But there was no time for questions. Alex joined them, leading the way through the heavy door that opened into the corridor.

"Come on, Jess." Malia grabbed Jess's arm. "Maybe we can help."

Jess was numb, but she followed Malia into the scene of utter destruction. The force of the tidal wave had diminished by the time it reached this spot, but even at that it had caused unbelievable havoc.

Inside the PR room Jess saw evidence that heavy desks and metal file cabinets had been flung against one wall, then sucked back toward the other wall. Water stood ankle deep on the floor, and here and there fish flopped about. Kelp twined its slimy tendrils about chairs and wastebaskets, and a putrid stench filled the room.

Jess slipped in the ooze and water, but Malia steadied her. Johnny led Alex to a far corner of the room, and for a moment Jess didn't see Reeta. Then, with a sickening realization, she made out her form lying partly submerged in kelp and ooze. Reeta's silvery hair and her usually spotlessly white outfit were now a greenish black, and her hands were covered with slime.

"Is she . . . dead?" Jess barely breathed the words.

"Let me see if I can feel a pulsebeat." Malia eased forward and picked up Reeta's limp wrist. As she did so, Jess saw the remains of a small tape recorder fall from Reeta's fingers. Jess's eye caught her father's just as Malia spoke.

"She's alive. I feel a weak pulse. Let's get her out of this filth. Up on a desk or something."

Alex and Johnny managed to drag a desk into an upright position. They wiped it off, then lifted Reeta onto it. At the movement, Reeta's eyelids opened, then closed again.

"She needs a doctor," Malia said. "And blankets. I think she's in shock. It's a miracle that she's alive."

As Jess inched closer to Reeta, Alex left the room, and Mr. Wong joined Jess.

"She must have come back here after office hours to get the recorder," Mr. Wong said. "I think we'll find a recording of your folktale on it, if I'm not mistaken."

Jess looked at the ruined recorder,

knowing nothing could have survived the force of the wave. When she glanced up, Reeta's eyes were open and she tried to speak.

"Bruce Brietag put me up to it, Jess. I'm sorry. Sorry. Bruce's brother . . . paid . . . big . . . money. Takes . . . money to be . . . in society."

"Don't try to talk, Reeta," Jess said. "The important thing is to get a doctor in here, to get you cleaned up. Your hands . . ."

"Hands are clean." Reeta murmured the words, then passed out again with her slime-smudged fingers relaxed on the desk top.

Jess looked at Reeta with pity instead of anger or resentment, and Mr. Wong shook his head sadly and covered Reeta with his sports coat.

There was little sleep that night. Hollow-eyed men and women tried to comfort their children, and a continuous stream of people appeared at the cannery seeking word of friends and relatives.

Hours passed before Alex appeared with a doctor, and more hours passed while they made the rounds of the ill and injured. It was almost dawn when Jess saw Alex sitting alone on the steps outside the cannery. She had done some serious thinking in the past hours. She had made some decisions, and now she knew what she must do.

Stepping out to where Alex sat, she eased down beside him. Removing the ring and its chain from her neck, she held it toward him.

"Alex, I can't wear this any longer. In all honesty and regret I must return it to you."

Alex's eyes widened. "What's the matter? What have I done?"

"You've done nothing except prove your bravery. I'm proud of you. Really proud."

"Then why are you returning my ring?"

"Because you deserve something better than I can offer at this time. I feel as if I've lived a lifetime in this endless, tragic night, Alex. But this disaster has brought me to my senses. Now I know exactly where I'm going, what I must do with my life."

"And your plans don't include marriage?"

"Not at the moment. I want to prove myself in a career, and the career I want is in public relations. I've decided tonight that it's the greatest field in the world. Tonight your first thought was to hurry here to help the cannery workers, and the cannery workers hurried here to help you. It was an exchange of goodwill. Why? Because in the past, through your job, through your original thinking, you have touched human lives in a meaningful and lasting way. This is the thing I want to be able to do."

"You flatter me," Alex said.

"It's the truth," Jess insisted. "But I'm looking at this situation realistically for the first time. Once I thought I could have everything all at once — husband, children, career. But now I know that's as impossible for me as it was for my mother. She and Dad had a good marriage until she changed, until she became successful in her own right."

"What difference did her success make?" Alex asked.

"Dad married her before she knew exactly what she wanted to do with her life. Then, gradually, she realized what she must do, that she must be an artist. Dad hadn't bargained for what he was getting. He simply couldn't adjust. I blame neither of them, but I don't want the same thing to happen to us, Alex."

"So you're giving up all thought of marriage?"

"Of course not. But I want my future husband to know me as a successful woman, not as an immature girl. That change may take a few years, but a good career plus a happy marriage will make the waiting worthwhile."

"There is no reason for me not to wait," Alex said.

"No," Jess said, smiling gently. "I'd like that."

As the sun rose, a truck eased up to the cannery bringing coffee and sandwiches, and Jess stepped forward to help distribute the food to the hungry. She smiled through her exhaustion. How ironic that it had taken a tidal wave to destroy her letter of resignation and to shock her into an awareness of herself and her relationship to others.

While Jess's hands were busy, her mind soared, and she remembered the words the personnel director had quoted from Huxley less than twenty-four hours ago. Jess still wasn't sure how she measured up to the ideal public relations worker, but she was determined to succeed. Through work and study she would magnify herself, she would multiply the ways in which she existed. And her relationship with Alex would grow. Her life would be full, significant, and interesting.